Everything will Fall into Place

Everything will Fall into Place

You are born to fly

Nipun Goel

genNEXT Publication

ISBN : 978-93-8022-288-2

Price : ₹ 180

First Published, 2016

Published by

Gennext Publications
5, Ansari Road
Daryaganj, New Delhi-110002
Phones: 9811692060
E-mail: gennext@hotmail.com

Printed at: G. Print Process, Delhi.

Cataloging in Publication Data—DK
Courtesy: D.K. Agencies (P) Ltd. <docinfo@dkagencies.com>

Goel, Nipun, author.
Everything will fall into place : You are born to fly / Nipun Goel.

pages cm
Novel.
ISBN 9789380222882

1. Fate and fatalism—Fiction. 2. Desire—Fiction. 3. Indic fiction (English) I. Title.

PR9499.4.G64E94 2015 DDC 823.92 23

Contents

Acknowledgement

I would like to express my gratitude to many people who saw me through this book. But firstly, I want to invariably thank my valuable reader and friend for choosing to read "*Everything will Fall into Place*".

As a reader for my first book, your support and trust in my ability to take you through a great journey while reading the book, which made you give your extremely precious time to me, matters a lot to me.

I have tried to enthuse my audience in the best possible way and promise to do so in the future. Entertaining you and passing on the little knowledge I have is my primary motive.

Here is thanking all those who provided constant support, talked things over, read, wrote, offered comments, assisted in proofreading and helped me with this book in some or the other way.

Above all, I would like to thank the mesmerising film industry globally, comprising of all the lovely actors and actresses for being an inspiration forever and thus help me write this book. Very few people realise this fact, but our adorable film-stars do the most courageous work of entertaining us in umpteen ways without any hesitation or thinking about the criticism by the Masses. Being a celebrity, they allow their lives to be in the limelight for various reasons always, which is not at all easy and something to take a bow to.

My charming parents, especially my loving mother, for her constant support while I was writing the book as well as reading the whole book page by page as I went ahead, providing important comments at every stage which helped me in writing the book properly.

My extremely talented sister Niharika, and my Neurologist-cum-Entrepreneur brother-in-law Dr Ketan, for reading the book at various stages and helping me with the structure of the book and pointing out some serious flaws in the initial story I had written, which made me devise a better book for my audience.

Those who helped me at various stages of conceptualising, marketing and proofreading - Megha, Namira, Priya, Nikita, Shweta, Auchitya and Shravil. My heartiest thanks to Megha for making me realise my capabilities as a writer, motivating me and being supportive throughout. Namira deserves a remarkable mention too for her consistent help at different stages of the book whenever needed.

Abhinav, his wife Shweta, Rashi and Ananya for their constant support in finalising the book title by regular brainstorming, providing valuable comments for the book after reading, and helping in the publishing process to proceed in the right way. Special thanks to Shikhar Mittal for his priceless hard work behind marketing videos and tips.

Last but not the least, I beg forgiveness of all those who have been with me during the course of the book and whose names I have failed to mention. All of my friends family have helped in some or the other way to reach where I am today and make me capable enough.

I apologise to every person, if any, who unfortunately gets hurt in any way after reading the book. The book is a complete work of fiction with fictitious characters, story and incidents. There is no intention to harm any personality or sentiment of any one in any way.

I want to reach out to as many people as I can, domestically as well as globally, and take them through a hilarious as well as philosophical journey always through any medium I wish to use. I believe in loving and be loved back. Henceforth, I just want your affection which will help me to improve for the better with a smile. I am not perfect, and will faulter, so I just request for your support throughout.

Nipun Goel

Everything will Fall into Place!

You are born to Fly

We often blame destiny for all the wrong that happens with us. What if, the same destiny takes us to the skies we could never imagine?

India is a country where people come together only to watch two things – Games or a Brawl. What if, the same people come together to watch us?

We move on in our lives dreaming about umpteen things and following various role models. What if, every dream we can ever think of becomes achievable and we become the role model of every aspiring person?

Welcome to "*Everything will Fall into Place*", a story of a guy who becomes one of the most eligible bachelor and a heart-throb at the age of just 23! The story depicts the role of destiny, hard work and the intensity with which something is desired in life. It is perfectly manifested in the case of "Gautam Kapoor – the Protaganist".

The story unveils the breath taking, motivating and exhilarating journey of this guy, who is not any prodigy, but sends a strong message at the end, that anything is possible, for everyone! The book depicts one of the biggest revelations ever possible to a huge population, where a totally unknown guy for the masses becomes one of the most eligible bachelors and a superstar overnight.

The book beautifully evinces the necessity of real perseverance and belief in what you desire, even if it seems impossible to achieve.

Although this philosophy has been preached for long, the book presents it with a remarkable impact.

Usually, there comes a high followed by a low in which one feels like everything is finished. But it is from there where the real rise starts. One needs to have that patience to wait for the opportunity and the strength to grab it at the right time to soar in life. Nothing comes for free in our journey to success. Someone or the other definitely puts in the hard work behind the grandeur engulfing anything.

The book consequently sends across the message that every person is indeed born to fly. The ones who don't have only one trait lacking in them which inhibits them from achieving what they desire- their true intentions behind it!

Prologue

"Am I in a dream?!!"

This line was reverberating in my mind again and again, as I stood on the stage with my hands spread out wide like the trademark style of India's best actor and superstar – Sameer Khan, and my closed eyes facing the sky. Sitting on the opposite side of the stage, were the who's who of the country and the whole film fraternity of India, a gathering one would rarely see together. They were all awestruck, and just shouting my name in ecstasy again and again. Yes, that was my charm today.

There were two big cylindrical-shaped sprinklers on my either side, throwing the most beautiful and colourful flowers out of them in the air at a high speed, which were ultimately falling on and all around me. The biggest film stars of the Indian Film Industry were hooting my name and champagne was being spilled all over the crowd in elation by my star friends. It was one of the biggest gatherings for any show ever, on the largest ground of Mumbai, with the most resplendent set of any stage show one could ever witness. Yes, it was not a dream any more.

"Thanks a bunch for so much love, each and every one of you", I said using the mike, enthralled to the core.

"Thanks a lot to my lovely family and friends for being supportive throughout, even though ninety nine per cent of them were unaware of the path I was treading on since the last six to seven years. I am delighted at the response from everyone out here, and I wouldn't have achieved this feat without the unseen blessings of all you lovely people".

As I took a pause owing to my speechlessness, which one usually witnesses in such kind of emotional moments, the crowd started cheering my name again. I was looking handsome and dapper in a luxurious velvet coat and pant. My perfectly toned and chiseled body could be clearly seen with only the coat over it.

All people across the country, and many across the globe would have been glued to their television screens since a couple of hours. Every channel of every category was broadcasting this event live, as arranged by the event management staff of this show.

I had spent hundreds of millions on just this one night of my life, a night which will transform me from a common man to one of the biggest celebrities.

This night had been my dream since I started my journey towards achieving this feat. I had always dreamt strongly about it even when I had not started working on it. I was getting jitters thinking about the mental state of everyone in my family, especially my parents. Till a few hours ago, they had been completely unaware about their son's achievement as I had been successful in hiding this secret for years. I had wanted to give this amazing gift to my parents with a bang.

As I signed off for the night, all the celebrities started coming and congratulating me one by one. The ones who were a part of this wonderful and interesting journey of mine came and hugged me, making me feel ecstatic. There were big politicians and industrialists as well at the event as they had been specially invited. They also came and congratulated me for the shocking piece of news that had got unveiled. I was declared the richest youngster of the country at such an age.

I had to leave immediately for my first home, Delhi, to where I belonged. I wanted to personally meet my parents as soon as possible.

I had narrated my whole journey from scratch in this event.

The people who knew me would have felt extreme emotions after getting to know the truth. Since they were unaware about this other side of Gautam Kapoor, would now have been able to co-relate all the cues.

As I left from the venue, I started getting nostalgic. There was a fleet of the most luxurious cars lined up for me to escort me to the airport. I sat in one of the cars, with the other cars around me as my security, and finally heaved a sigh of relief. I needed some time alone. I started remembering every part of this glorious journey of mine, which had only been possible owing to my truest desire to become what I did today.

My eyes had a bit of numbness as I mused about what I had lost on my way up the ladder. The cars started moving, and so did my memories.

1

Every Passion demands Madness

I was born and brought up in a well-off family, but that was the case with numerous people out there too. I was a hard working student in my school days, and I had my focus only on academics, which was reflected in my top grades throughout my school life. I always took less interest in other stuff like bunking of classes, hanging out with friends and extra-curricular activities.

We all start weaving numerous dreams since childhood, with the dreams getting re-shaped or changed every now and then with the passage of time. We dream of various materialistic desires, things that interest us and places where we wish to see ourselves in life. It is a common saying that one should have an aim as sharp as that of Arjuna, one of the most famous characters of the major epic Mahabharata. The good part in my case was that I was always focused on one single dream and toiled day and night to achieve it. I felt proud thinking this, and I sat in a bit more relaxed way in my limousine. I lit a cigarette, pinched myself to make sure that this day was real, and started thinking again about my journey. I knew that my ride till my private jet standing at the airport would be a bit longer than usual, owing to the traffic of Mumbai.

During the early days of my childhood, I used to believe that I would have to join my dad's business. Usually, a child hailing from a business family is expected to ultimately join the family business. But as I matured, I realised that my heart belonged somewhere else.

The Bollywood industry had always fascinated me head over heels. I was a movie buff throughout, and used to adore all the film stars in various roles. I used to listen to film music every day, as it made me feel at ease. With the passage of time, that desire and passion to be like these film stars started building inside me as a must-have in life: to be cheered and adored by all, have girls go crazy for you, and earn at a pace no one can imagine. However, I knew that this life which the film stars lived was not a cakewalk. It had been bestowed on them owing to their hard work and struggle, because nothing comes free in life. I had always been a good poet and writer, and I gradually started dreaming of writing songs and movie scripts, even though a part of my heart always knew that all this was a far-fetched dream.

In India, most of the people feel helpless while pursuing any kind of work without contacts. Bollywood is no different. I did not have the option of going to Mumbai as a struggler as I knew that my family would definitely find it unrealistic and would not allow me to do so. Fighting with them would have yielded no results because of the extremely low probability of selection. The probability was low owing to the lacking of a strong backing.

But still, the hidden desire of being associated with the film industry grew stronger by leaps and bounds with every passing day. I never stopped getting mesmerised by the love showered upon the big film stars by people. I myself never hesitated in showing my deepest affection for these ideal role models.

Whenever I took a break from studies during school days, I wrote songs and poems in a notebook, which became very dear to me since the day I started writing in it. I craved to fly to Mumbai, the home of the Bollywood industry, and show this book as soon as possible to the best producers or directors of the industry to promptly get selected. But usually this visualising session was followed by a hearty laugh at my own self as I knew there must be people better than me already present there. However, I avoided under-estimating myself too much, which turned out to be a big positive in my case.

It instilled in me a feeling of being worthy enough to be there amongst the already established script writers and lyricists. Time passed by, and I entered the eleventh standard of my school. This was the game-changing year of my life, the year I can never forget. It presented me with the base of my career, which is at an unprecedented height today.

The happenings with me during this year made me realise the real inception of destiny and God in my life. I firmly started believing that our desires do have the power to shape our destiny accordingly, provided they don't get deterred or reshaped come what may. It is important to have a true desire for one single thing in life. God will always give an opportunity to fulfil such a desire, but then it is in our hands how we utilise that opportunity and put in the hard work. The trueness of my desire to become a loved celebrity, and be able to live life totally on my own terms had always been unaffected by all the other happenings of my life. Even though I never found any way out to follow that path, the fire to be that imaginary Gautam Kapoor was always burning in my belly with the same intensity. Such is the real test of a desire, wherein despite the fact that the desire seems unachievable, the life in that desire is always kept alive.

"Gautam, is that you?", my mom said in a high pitched tone, as I entered my home from a routine day at school, during the beginning of my eleventh standard.

"Yes mom, it's me. Please give me my lunch fast. I am too hungry", I said, gasping, as I ran towards my room to change, with hunger bells ringing in my stomach.

My favourite pass time was to get glued to the television as soon as I came back from school, and watch and shuffle between various movies being run on different channels. It had become a sort of necessity for me, since I could not digest my food without a movie playing in front of my eyes.

I also used to repeatedly watch the latest trailers of upcoming movies on YouTube, a video sharing website and get inspired to do something significant enough for the whole world to recognise me. This was a daily affair owing to my extreme love for this industry. I had a firm belief that the primary aim of all people belonging to the film fraternity was to entertain their fans. Despite the immense hard work which was put in for this purpose, their actions were sometimes misinterpreted and labelled as controversial, materialistic or illegal.

I still maintain that it is a common phenomenon to degrade a person or a group that garners money and fame. However, one should turn a deaf ear to such criticism and it should not become a deterrent in one's journey towards one's goal.

2

Respect every Female; She is your true mentor

Eleventh standard is usually a class where the jump from the tenth standard in terms of academic difficulty is quite high, resulting in a drop of grades. Along with that, we enter a different category of maturity and our passions shift towards partying, drinking, dating and other such activities. I had a similar kind of influence, and from a nerd, I slowly got transformed to a flirt and an extrovert. Since the sections had got shuffled in the eleventh standard, I got the opportunity to meet new people and interact with them. The same happened during tuitions, which were imperative due to difficulty in studies as well as graduation admissions ahead.Thus, I was gradually able to give a diversified and holistic approach to my personality and become street smart.

When you meet more people, you get to know how different they can be, both in a good and bad way. That enables you to imbibe the good qualities and refrain from the bad ones. One day at my tuition, a guy came dressed up in yellow coloured pants and a pink coloured shirt. Over such an amazing blend of fashion, he was wearing pointed blue coloured shoes with the 'Jaguar' logo protruding out from both, replicating the logo of the 'Jaguar' brand of automobiles.

I was in splits. But that guy was confident and unperturbed by the silent criticism he garnered from the class. That was the positive to learn from this incident. Imbibing every bit of the reel industry's fashion trend in real life is foolishness, was the negative to learn.

Having a record of being a studious and obedient child, I used to get permissions easily from my parents for going to late night parties as well getting to drive the car alone. Having a car to myself was the best way to live a crazy life, and have more freedom to do certain things demanding restrictions otherwise. I had started enjoying my life in a different way now, but I had always done everything in limits in order to maintain my parents' trust and have a feel good factor.

Arush, one of my best friends in school, had a similar nature as mine. Maybe that was the reason that we guys clicked together in a brilliant way.

I used to discuss a lot of things with him.I had one sister who was a couple of years elder to me. She was pursuing her graduation.

It was just another day when Arush and me were sitting in the class and chatting.

"Gautam, there is a party at my friend's house this Saturday night. You also come along with me. It would be a lot of fun", Arush said.

"Oh really! That is so interesting. Yes, I will definitely come", I said, totally excited.

"That friend of mine is a rich brat. He knows some of the celebrities too. You may spot a couple of them there", Arush said, with a wink.

"How come he knows celebrities at such an age? And so much so that they would be visiting him for his party too?", I asked, smelling some fishiness as well as getting jealous.

"Dude! His dad is a big industrialist who has a fat bank account. He knows a lot of celebrities since he sponsors a lot of events and award functions in Mumbai", Arush said.

I got more excited hearing this, owing to my fascination for the film industry. I started waiting eagerly for the party. On the day of the party, Arush had told me to get a pack of cigarettes along with me. I had kept it in my coat's outer pocket while getting ready. As I entered my parents' bedroom to take the car keys and say goodbye to them, the car keys fell on the floor. I bent to pick up the keys and totally forgot about the cigarettes in my pocket. They fell from my coat on the floor just next to my hand as I held the car keys to pick them up. I was petrified.

I was sure when I would turn my head above, four eyes would be staring at me in repugnance. I started chanting God's name and slowly started standing straight from the bent down position, so that I could think of an idea by then.

"Oh my God!", I exclaimed.

"This pack of cigarettes was in my coat's pocket?! I will just inform my friend Rahul about his packet which he gave to me last week in a party to keep, but forgot to take it back", I said, in total confidence, wanting my parents to hear properly whatever I was saying. I took out my phone and acted that I have dialled a number and started talking.

"Hey Rahul. How are you? Dude I finally found your pack of cigarettes, which you had given to me at the party last week. I had no clue that I had kept it in my coat's pocket. I am so sorry. I will return it to you tomorrow in school", I said. Somehow I had managed to act well, and look confident, making my parents totally change that repulsive look they would have had at the moment the pack had fallen.

"Gautam, your friends' smoke too?!", my mom asked me, with a horrified look on her face.

"That too at such an early age?". I tried to compose myself and not show any nervousness.

"Yes mom. Some of them do. But it is their life. I am away from these bad habits mom", I said quickly, kissed on my mother's forehead and left the room, to avoid any further discussion. I heaved a big sigh of relief as I left the house and thanked God. Although I did not use to smoke regularly, I had tried it a couple of times at parties with friends. Arush also used to smoke occasionally at parties, but as an effort to look sophisticated, he preferred carrying a box rather than loose cigarettes. I supported him in his immature thinking.

I reached the party venue. The magnificence of the party could be witnessed from the decoration and lighting of the bungalow from outside. Arush came down to receive me since he had reached a little earlier.

"Vow man! It seems like a grand party even from outside", I said to Arush.

"You look dressed like an actor, my hero".

"Thanks brother. Yes, the party is grand surely. You will see the real grandeur once you enter inside Gautam", Arush said, looking electrified already.

As I entered the party, Arush made me meet his friend who had hosted the party. The party looked more lavish than I had imagined. The crowd was amazing, with proper catering, music, dance floor and lightings in place. As I decided to take a round through the party, in order to have a quick glance at all the people and happenings there, I spotted a couple of famous actresses. I was mesmerised. I so wanted to be capable enough to stand amongst them too. I could only dream though.

"Ahem Ahem! I can see where your eyes are looking Gautam", Arush whispered in my ears from behind, since he must have spotted me standing there.

"No, I am just adoring them Arush", I said.

"You would obviously! Do you want to go and get a photograph clicked with them?", Arush asked me.

"No no! I am not dying to have photographs with them", I said, even though I badly was.

"You know Akshay would also be coming for this party", Arush said, and started laughing. I looked at him with disgust.

"I know you told this to me deliberately, as you know I even hate hearing his name", I said, making serious facial expressions.

"Really! I did not know that", Arush said, winking and giggling.

"He hasn't returned your money yet?"

"No, but he remembers that he has to give me the money he borrowed from me", I said, and we both started laughing together.

"Hey Gautam, I have to give you back those two thousand bucks I borrowed from you. I would give them to you very soon as I don't have enough cash right now, but I just intend to tell you that I remember very clearly", Arush said, dubbing in Akshay's voice, who was a common school friend of ours.

Arush also couldn't control laughing while saying so, and I could also just laugh it out, as I had been hearing this line from Akshay since the past three months.

"Anyways, come I will make you meet some good girls here", Arush said. I hugged him in delight. Arush graciously changed my mood.

He took me to a group of people standing there, which was perhaps his group other than school, with whom he used to hang out and party frequently. He introduced me one by one to all his friends. There were some girls who were really pretty in that group.

Owing to my good observation power, I had seen a girl using Tinder in the party on her phone. Tinder was a mobile application, which used to show all the registered people on its network in the location range set by us. We had to like the photograph of the person we liked, and in case the same person liked our photograph, it used to generate a match.

I remembered that I had installed the application some days ago when someone was telling about it but had not quite used it. I quickly opened it and set my location search range to one kilometre. I knew that girl would surely come in the search quickly then. I liked her picture as soon as I spotted it. Now the wait was for her to do the same once she opens the application again. To my delight, she did open and like my photograph. I got a notification that very moment and I was on cloud nine seeing that. I quickly turned up to search for her. She was standing in one corner looking at me and waiting for me to look at her as soon as I see the notification. I went to her finally to talk.

"Hi, I am Gautam Kapoor", I said to her, with my confidence building up.

"Hello. I am Devika Goel. I must say you are a smart guy", she said, looking impressed. It gave me a boost.

"So what do you do?", I asked, with my mind running at unpredictable speed to ask the best questions and not leave any bad impression.

"I am in my twelfth standard, studying in Delhi Public School", she said.

"Oh that's great! I am in the eleventh standard. It is a good coincidence that we both are in school", I said, just spitting out whatever I could think of. But she did give it a laugh, and I was successful with my crappy lines. I decided to ask her out for a dance now, but as soon as I gathered the guts to do so, I was shocked at what happened next.

Deepika Sanon, one of the actresses present at the party, and the new reigning queen of the Bollywood industry, came up to where I was standing. My eyes were constantly staring at her now, but she did not look at me even once. She started talking to Devika, oblivious of my presence just next to her. It was indeed the first time I was standing just next to an actress, even though like a complete stranger. My mind had totally diverted from Devika to my dream world of the film industry and I was lost looking at the gorgeous actress.

"I would be leaving in another ten minutes. I have a flight to catch to Mumbai. It was lovely hanging out with you on this short trip", the actress said to Devika.

"Ah that is so sweet of you Deepika. I had an amazing time with you too. I would miss you. Come I will drop you till your car", Devika said, holding her hand as they walked towards the exit of the hall, to the car parking outside the house. I was awestruck, which could be attributed to a couple of reasons.

I stood next to one of the best actresses of the Indian film industry. Apparently, the girl who liked me on Tinder seemed like a close friend or relative of such a famous actress. The way the two conversed reflected a good relationship between them. I was standing like a frozen statue at that place.

"Gautam, come let's dance with other people", Arush said to me after a while of searching for me. I didn't give any reaction. Arush waived his hand in front of my face and repeatedly took my name.

I told Arush about Devika after I got back to my senses. He told me to not let the opportunity go and impress her totally.

"Hey Gautam! I am back. Sorry for leaving in between", Devika said.

"It is alright Devika. Would you like to have a dance with me?", I said, instantly kneeling down on my knees. Devika got shocked and started looking here and there. Arush turned his face in the opposite direction to dissociate himself from what had just happened and portray as if he did not know me. I was unmoved though, and kept being in that position looking into Devika's eyes.

I didn't know from where had I gathered so much guts but I stuck to what I did and remained confident. I remembered the confidence level of that tuition mate of mine who had come dressed as a total disaster one day. My passion to get close to Devika surely worked out, and maybe to make things seem normal, Devika held my hand and quickly took me to the dance floor. Nothing comes easy. My continuous work towards improving my personality day by day and my confidence level were the reasons behind wooing Devika.

I held her by her back and we started dancing on slow music in a romantic way.

"Do you know you are really mad?", Devika said softly, not seeming perturbed by that fact though. I could sense that things were working out for me. I had a sweet smile on my face, with dimples shining prominently on both my cheeks.

"Oh! You look so cute when you smile", Devika added.

"Thanks a ton dear. You add to my cuteness perhaps", I murmured, unsure whether to really try getting this much cheesy. But to my surprise, Devika smiled and gave me an indication of already being lured by my tactics.

"Can I ask you something?", I said.

"Yes sure", Devika said.

"How do you know that famous actress Deepika who just came and talked to you. I hope she was the same personality and not her duplicate", I said, laughing a bit.

"Yes, she was real and the same actress you are thinking about", Devika said, smiling back.

"I know her because my mom hails from Mumbai, and coincidently she has been a very good friend of Deepika's mother as they used to live in the same society. Me and Deepika are childhood friends consequently. I always meet her whenever I visit Mumbai to my maternal side relatives if she is free and in the city, and vice versa", she said.

"Wow! You are such a lucky girl. I wish my parents also had such childhood friends", I said, chuckling, with my love for such celebrities being a bit visible.

I danced more with Devika, trying to look better and charming to her. I did not know what my true feelings were, but I just knew that Devika was a beautiful girl with whom I wanted to spend quality time, with her indirect Bollywood connection being an icing on the cake. I noted down her mobile number before Arush and I left from the party.

"It calls for a grand celebration my boy", Arush shouted, as soon as we left from the party, totally happy for the winner in me tonight.

"You deserve it brother! Thanks for getting me along to a wonderful party", I said. It was around midnight when we left, and Arush was sleeping over at my place tonight.

"You are a stud Gautam. Hats off to your tactics. You got the best, trust me", Arush said.

"Yes buddy. I am really happy. I don't know from where I garnered all the courage to do whatever I did tonight, and luckily everything worked in my favour", I said, delighted.

"Ok brother, control your excitement. There are police check posts ahead. Although we have not drank much, we need to be calm and composed in front of them and not look suspicious", Arush said, with a sudden change of tone. But I was lost in my own world. I was truly happy. Suddenly a very peppy dance number started playing on the radio, and I couldn't control my urge to dance as soon as the police stopped us for the routine check.

I turned the volume up, got off my car, and started dancing on the road, forcing the policeman to dance along. Arush held his head in shock with both his hands, and instantly got off the car.

"Sir, we are really sorry. He is not drunk. He just had a very great night, and that is why he is on cloud nine. Kindly excuse us", Arush told the policeman in a sweet childish manner, making the policeman somewhat believe him and forgive me. Arush forcibly put me back in the car, and drove my car to my home for the rest of the way.

"Control your emotions Mr Playboy", Arush said to me. We reached home soon.

"Dude! She must be on your Facebook profile right, as she is also a part of your clubbing group?", I asked Arush, as soon as I entered my room.

"Yes I suppose, although we never interacted much", Arush said.

"Open it quickly. I want to check her pictures out", I said, in excitement. Coincidently, she was doing the same at that time. Suddenly a message popped on my phone, which surprisingly was from Devika. I got overwhelmed as well as curious. Arush too asked me the reason behind my excitement and we both read the message together after I opened it.

"Hey Gautam. It was wonderful meeting you today. I was just scrolling through your Facebook profile right now and trying to know you a bit more. Facebook was one of the biggest social media networking websites. You look really cute in a lot of pictures of yours. I must say you have an impressive personality", the text message from Devika read so. Arush and I, both looked at each other's face Arush started laughing hard.

"Cute pictures and an impressive personality. I never noticed these qualities in you dude", Arush said, trying to control his laughter more since I had started blushing also.

"It's not funny Arush! Anyway, I will start going to the garden for jogging from tomorrow. Beautiful girls come there to jog everyday. You should come along and find one for yourself too", I said, with a manifestation of the king type feeling I was getting at that moment.

"I know many other strategies to grab a girl's attention in the jogging park. So I can really help you out", I added.

"You don't need to act so stylish by wooing one girl Gautam. She can leave you too after she starts knowing you more", Arush said, with good chuckles.

"You are so funny Arush! On a serious note, I would help you in doing that. It would be a fun thing to do, and maybe you really find one for yourself", I said.

"Okay dude. I can bank on you for this I guess", Arush said. We slept off in a while. I preferred to reply to Devika the next morning, in order to not show any desperateness.

For the next few days we used to go regularly to the park and observe the girls who were regular visitors too. Arush liked one girl finally, who seemed to be sweet and family oriented. The other day when she came for a walk in the garden, I told Arush to bring one small child along with him, from the ones who used to sit outside the temple adjacent to the park to beg for food and money. It was a part of my plan to make Arush date that girl he had started liking. The child was fair and cute whom Arush had selectively picked, and I gave him some money to do my work.

As soon as that girl crossed a pre decided landmark in the park, that child started crying mercilessly, as per my instructions. Arush was walking a little ahead of the girl, which was also planned. I had told Arush to pretend and stop while walking in front of the girl when he spots that child and kneel down to wipe his tears.

"What happened dear? Why are you crying?", Arush said to that beggar child, in the sweetest possible voice. I was trying to control my laughter seeing his acting, hiding behind a bush. Arush took him in his arms, and was aware that the girl would be watching everything from behind. Arush had utilised the distance he had kept between her to make her see and understand the situation vividly. The boy continued crying as per my instructions. The girl stopped there too as soon as she reached that spot, a few minutes after Arush had stopped.

"What happened? Why is this cute child crying", the girl said to Arush.

"I don't know! I also just spotted him on the jogging track. I guess he has lost his parents", Arush said, in a very innocent way to the girl. My heart was dancing from inside seeing this newly found camaraderie.

"Come let us search for his parents then", the girl said to Arush. Arush was delighted, and agreed to that. He looked at me stealthily and winked. The girl and Arush, along with the child, then started taking a round of the garden to search for his family. Arush pretended not to show any interest in the girl in order to portray himself as a genuine and innocent guy. It was my turn now to give the climax to the plan. I came out of the bush and started walking in the opposite direction of Arush's, in order to meet him and the girl on the way.

The boy got off from Arush's arms and ran towards me as soon as he saw me. He had a thirty two teeth grin on his face, for which I had promised to pay him extra. I went and thanked the girl for taking care of the child telling her that he was my younger brother and had ran away while playing on the ground.

"No please don't thank me for this. It is all because of him", the girl said, pointing towards Arush. Everything was working exactly as per my plan and Arush's eyes were beaming.

"No please don't embarrass me mam. You were walking all along to help this child. I can't take the credit alone", Arush said, again in the politest voice.

"Oh my God! Please don't call me mam. My name is Ketki", she said.

"Well, thanks a ton to both of you. We rarely see people like you nowadays. May God bless you both always", I said, controlling my laughter. Perhaps Arush was also controlling his laughter on my last line. I went away with the child from there. My work had been done, and now was Arush's turn to utilise the situation and get talking with the girl he had just impressed.

"That was really sweet of you to give me the credit as well. What is your name?", Ketki said.

"I just said what the truth was, Ketki. I hope you don't mind calling me by your name. My name is Arush", he said.

"We can walk and talk if you are fine with it. Yes, you should call me by my name only", she said. Arush wanted to start dancing hearing so from Ketki herself.

"Yes that's a great idea. So what do you do?", Arush said, with a sweet baby-like smile permanently there on his face till they talked. The general talks continued, and he finally noted down Ketki's mobile number before leaving, which was now a very easy task for him.

"Thanks buddy! I don't know what I will do without you. You are indeed so smart", Arush called me up and told me.

"I am always there buddy. No thanks please. See I promised you that I would hook you up with someone too. You would have taken her mobile number obviously. Now gradually start luring her towards you more and more", I said.

"Sure Gautam. I will see you in school tomorrow buddy. My mom is calling me", Arush said, and hung up.

3

Don't be Blind to genuine people in your Life

I also remembered suddenly that my mom was calling me too a while ago. I went to my parent's room and as soon as I entered their room, I saw them chuckling with their eyes glued at the idiot box. They were watching the iconic show "Comedy Nights with Kapil", which had gained immense popularity in the country. In today's world, this show was a barometer to measure the popularity and success of a person, as being invited to the show usually depicted in itself about the person being successful. I had a strong feeling and desire that someday when I enter the film industry and become famous, I would also be invited to the show. I shunned my extra ordinary thoughts suddenly.

"Hey mom, you called me?", I said.

"Yes son. I have a good news for you", my mom said, sounding elated.

"What mom? Tell me quickly", I said, thinking in all possible directions as to what the news could be related to.

"We all will have to go to USA for attending Rashi's wedding. She got engaged", my mom said.

"Oh really! Oh! That is so awesome! When do we have to go?", I said with great enthusiasm. I had just heard that part of mom's line which said about our trip to USA and had totally unheard the engagement of a first cousin of mine staying in the States.

"We have to leave next month. We will get the tickets booked as soon as possible and apply for the Visa", mom said.

"You can afford to miss your school right?"

"Yes my dear mom. I am not in the twelfth standard right now. I will have board exams next year", I said. I was really thankful to God that I was indeed in the eleventh standard. Had I been in the twelfth standard, I would have not been able to go for the trip. I had a new thing to look forward to, owing to my inclination towards travelling, airports and adventure.

"Hey. How you doing?", a message popped on my phone as I came to my room joyous. The message was from Devika. I guess whenever we are happy, good things tend to happen more with us. That is why it is always advised to be happy in life no matter what the situation is, in order to attract positive powers.

"Hello Devika. I am doing well. You tell what is going on at your end? I was thinking of messaging you only right now", I messaged back.

"I am busy with my studies, she said.

"Was that inclination towards me in the party just fake?", she sent another message saying so.

"Yes I have been busy in some work too. We will meet soon. No Devika, there is nothing like that. I have been missing you all this while, but was preoccupied in various things", I said. I was deliberately not showing much interest to her, in order to garner more attention from her, and wait for the right time to show my emotional side. But I always made a point that I never treat any girl badly.

I met Devika the next day at a coffee shop. She was looking more beautiful than before. The excitement of going to the United States had not sunk in me yet, thus I seemed very ecstatic.

"Hey Gautam. How are you doing? Finally I get the chance to meet a busy personality", Devika said as she saw me waiting at a table when she entered the coffee shop. Sarcasm could easily be sensed in her tone.

"It's nothing like that Devika. You know how much school sucks and the pressure of assignments in eleventh standard", I said. She nodded, since she had no answer to my statement. I had decided to tell her about my USA trip next month, but I suddenly thought of another plan to make her fall totally in love with me. I had started liking her, and I thought that it was the perfect time to play the next set of tactics.

"So what else do you do besides school", Devika said.

"Hey I need to go. I will talk to you later. I am sorry", I said spontaneously and gloomily, and left from there, walking swiftly. Devika stood up totally shocked for a moment. Anyone would have wondered the reason behind such a rude and impromptu behaviour. I went home and started working on my laptop for implementing the plan I had thought of. I was good at photography and using a couple of photography softwares. I downloaded some pictures of Devika from her Facebook profile and replaced the face of one of the girls besides me in different photographs of mine with that of Devika's. I comfortably relaxed on my bed after that, with the phone in my hand, my eyes on its screen and a countdown starting in my mind. Within a couple of minutes, I got a message from Devika, exactly like I had visualised.

"Hey Gautam. I am sorry if I seem like a pile on to you. I found your behaviour very strange and rude today", Devika said, on the message.

"Hello Devika. It is me who should say sorry for my callous behaviour today. I cannot hide the reality anymore. I am sending you some photographs which would clear the air of my inhibition", I said. I sent her the photographs, which I had edited. Besides that, I had surfed Google properly over the recent air crashes. I was now waiting for her message eagerly.

"Oh my God! What is this Gautam? I cannot believe my eyes. Numerous questions are revolving in my mind! I guess you would be able to clear all those better by telling everything", Devika's message read.

"I really wanted to call you as soon as I saw the photographs, but my mom is present at home and my reactions over the phone would definitely make her suspicious", another message dropped in from Devika just after the last one.

"I am sure you must be shocked. I was also shocked when I saw you for the first time at that party. I guess God had made me attend it only to make me meet you. I did not have the guts to tell you anything in that party that night and I did everything in a state of disbelief", I said, in the message.

"I had a girl friend who looked exactly the same as you. We were like the happiest couple. And the fatal Delhi-bound plane crash last year finished it all! I have mixed feelings when I meet or talk to you although it has been almost negligible till now. It's better we don't talk Devika. I am sorry for troubling you", I said, making myself sound as gloomy as possible. She didn't reply anything to it, as I had expected. I was prepared for a call from her in a couple of days.

I diverted my mind towards my trip thereafter, and started helping my dad in all the work related to the trip from application of visa, booking of tickets to the preparation of a complete checklist for the trip and planning out the process to complete all the jotted down tasks. I had always loved to behave in a way different from all others, show immaturity at times and always attract people's attention towards me in some or the other way. Consequently the other day in school, as the class was proceeding in a boring way, I decided to break the ice by asking questions from the teacher again and again by listening in the class for a change. The whole class was shocked and my friends were continuously looking at me and giggling seeing my dedication.

I left with Arush after the school got over for home as he had got his car. We decided to buy a beer from the wine shop and have it in the car on the way back. As I sat, relaxed on the seat and was just going to open the bottle of beer, I heard a sound of someone shouting.

"Hey! You silly little boy wearing a white shirt!", a voice was coming from my left side. It was the voice of a fat uncle sitting in his car. I turned around suddenly.

"Are you talking to me?", I asked, looking at that uncle with a sort of disgust and a frown. His eyes seemed like that of a drowsy person with a kind of eagerness in them.

"Yes son. I am talking to you", he said. I made a weird facial expression smelling something fishy.

"I have a humble request. You look like a school going boy and you are inculcating these bad habits. You have a long life ahead of you son", he added. I interrupted him.

"Are you the father of a church?", I said, pretending to pay serious attention to his talks and deciding to take the case of the uncle in return.

"No my child. I am just advising you to leave these bad habits. Just throw this bottle", he said, very politely. I was finding him very weird for sure.

"Okay uncle. I will definitely heed your advice. Thanks for enlightening me", I said, making a puppet face, and turned my face towards Arush all of a sudden, murmuring to him to start the car and move from there. That uncle was irritating me now and I was getting furious.

"Son! Since you have agreed to throw the bottle off the car, I will advice you to give it to me. You should not litter the roads too. I will throw it in a safe way", he said. The eagerness to get the beer could easily be witnessed in his eyes and talks now. I understood the whole plot and thought of making some profit in lieu of his blabbering till now. I gathered that he was unaware that there was a wine & beer shop right behind the building in front of us, and we being aware of every nook and corner of the place knew this area properly.

"My dear uncle! I will leave this habit for sure. But I want to get a bottle of coke and some good food from that shop over there so that I get used to good habits. Can you give me some money in place of this bottle?", I said, very softly, making fun of that person inside my heart.

"Yes dear, for sure. How much is the bottle for?", said the uncle. He sounded so happy as if he had won the World Cup, but was unaware that we were the ones indeed who will cheer more than him in a while.

"Uncle, the bottle is for three hundred Rupees", I said.

"What?! So costly?", the uncle said, and burped. I believed he had already digested half the beer after hearing the price.

"Yes uncle. The proprietor of the wine shop told me that I am underaged for drinking and would be given this alcohol only for such a high price. Now I don't have any money left too", I said, pretending to be gloomy.

"Where is that wine shop you got this beer from?", the uncle said.

"I forgot the way uncle. I am so sorry. I am not that good at remembering ways. I just keep on going wherever the way takes me uncle", I said, sounding like a cute greedy child asking for a box full of chocolates. The uncle agreed as his greed for the beer was more than the worth of that bottle, and my trick had worked. He handed over the money and went away happily. I was much happier than he was, and as soon as he went away, I got out of the car and got five bottles of beer from the wine and beer shop.

"Cheers brother!", I said to Arush.

"We can keep the stock and have next time".

"This is crazy brother. Great going", Arush said, and we both burst into laughter.

We went back home with cheerful faces bitching about that uncle. I went back home, changed and thought of sleeping for a bit. I was in the middle of my sleep, as well as a beautiful dream. I was in a dream where I had become a big celebrity in the Bollywood industry. The dream engulfed the night of my birthday, wherein I had thrown a grand party for all the film fraternity, my family and friends. All the who's who of the industry were present at my party along with a live media coverage. I was greeting all the celebrities, with everyone having a lot of fun. All the gorgeous ladies present over there were swiped away by my charm and hospitality.

I was so happy with such a height of illusion that I even started smiling while sleeping. Suddenly my phone rang out loud, and I woke up from this sublime dream. I got annoyed, and picked my phone in haste with a feeling of thrashing the caller through the phone. It was Devika's phone. My anger turned into calmness all of a sudden, since I knew this call was really important.

I picked up the call, and utilising my already sleepy voice, I pretended to sound low.

"Hey Gautam. How are you?", Devika said, with a soft voice. I was convinced that she had been touched emotionally. I was a bit embarrassed for the lies I had told to her hearing her gloomy voice, but I thought that this age is such that all guys tend to do so. But I had also started developing feelings for her at the same time, and wanted to date her by giving my hundred per cent. I had consequently convinced myself that whatever I had done was not totally immoral since my future intentions were not bad.

"Hello Devika. How are you? I am good. How come you called?", I said, sounding more low than she was and a bit shocked at the same time.

"Are you fine Gautam? You sound very low. I am getting worried", she said.

"No please don't worry Devika. Yes I am feeling a bit down since a couple of days. I was craving to talk to you all this while, but was feeling guilty", I said.

"No Gautam! Why are you feeling guilty? You have done the most wonderful thing by expressing the truth. I adore you. I want to confess something to you", she said. Happiness ran from the top of my spine to the bottom of my body. My lips were not ready to deprive themselves of that smile. I controlled myself.

"Yes Devika. Thanks a ton for understanding. It means a lot to me. You can say whatever you want to freely", I said.

"Gautam! I really like you. I don't know what you feel for me. But I have really started falling for you. I was shocked seeing and hearing about the story of your ex-girlfriend who resembled me in every way. I guess God has sent me in your life again to fill her space only", she said, getting more and more emotional after every line. I started getting goose bumps now. I could feel the trueness in her talks.

"Devika! I am so touched. I really believe you are right! God has done this intentionally only. Maybe you are a different person from the one I knew before, but I am sure you are no less than a gem like she was. I like you too Devika", I said.

"Oh! That is so sweet of you to say so. I am really excited and happy. I am sorry to have expressed this all on the phone, but was not able to gather the strength to meet and say", she said.

"I understand Devika. I am so glad you called. I appreciate your courage. I am so blessed to have you in my life. Let's meet soon please", I said, with a lot of eagerness.

"Okay dear. I will come wherever you tell me to", she said, shying and smiling a bit. I punched my fist with a thrust in the air feeling elated. I told her to meet me today itself for dinner, and I booked a romantic restaurant in Delhi for my first dinner date and started getting ready with a lot of excitement and spruceness, as If I was getting married tonight. I had to lie to my mom saying that it was Arush's birthday party tonight. I had informed him about the whole situation too, so that he could handle in case anything goes wrong.

I reached the venue where I had called Devika. It was an open air restaurant, decorated beautifully all over for lightening the love of all the couples there. A live band was playing the most romantic instrumental songs of veteran Hindi Film singers. The weather was pleasant and windy. It was the perfect romantic moment to meet your special one. I went and sat at the table, which I had already reserved, and started waiting for Devika. Suddenly I saw a person entering the restaurant, wearing a lovely red dress, and looking as pretty as one could. She looked at me with all the love possible, and ran up to hug me.

"I am so happy to see you Devika", I said, hugging her. I truly felt on the top of the world. I was not sure I loved her or not, but at that particular moment, it seemed more than love to me. I just wanted to give her all the happiness I could for the time we spend together ahead.

"Aww! That is so sweet of you Gautam. I have surely fallen for you. You are my rock-star baby", she said. I looked into her eyes and she did the same after we hugged. We both were craving to kiss each other, and she gathered the courage this time to give a quick peck, as we both knew we were in a public place. She sat down and smiled so beautifully after that short kiss that I just felt like continuously looking at her. I held her hand over the table, looked above at the sky, and thanked God for the wonderful gift. I was really happy. We had a wonderful time talking to each other. I told her everything that was there in my heart and thought it was the right time to brief her with my passion for becoming a celebrity and doing some remarkable work in the Bollywood industry.

"Do you know what attracted me at the first place so much to you Devika?", I said to her, as she was sitting all lost in me.

"No dear. Please enlighten me on that. I would love to hear whatever you will tell", she said, softly. These extra cheesy lines were definitely giving me an adrenaline rush.

"Oh! That is so sweet. To tell you, when I saw you with the famous actress Deepika Sanon that night at the party, I really got attracted to you more. That is because the film industry and their fraternity have always captivated me. I never told you but I have always wanted to do something big in this line of work only", I said, feeling a bit shy. Devika laughed a bit, as expected.

"Really?! I appreciate your candidness Gautam. I promise you that whenever she comes here next time, I will make you meet her", she said.

"Vow! I would love that. I wish you could talk to her about letting me get some work to do also. You know I have a diary where I keep writing songs, articles, stories all the time, thinking that someday, maybe, it gets me a fortune", I said, with a seriousness in my talks. Devika's facial expressions manifested clearly that she understood my desire and passion. The way she was looking at me gave me a really good feeling, and that was enough for me to get contended, as I knew it somewhere in my heart that these talks are only superficial and next to impossible to get real. Devika also did not comment much on that as she would also have felt the same. We spent some more quality time together talking on various topics.

I went back home after dropping Devika and called Arush.

"Arush my dear! I am formally in a relationship now brother. I had my first official date tonight", I said, screaming happily on the phone.

"Oh really! I already knew this is bound to happen", he said.

"Yes brother. I am really happy. Devika is an amazing girl", I said.

"Great man! I am really happy for you both. God bless you guys always", he said.

"Come-on brother! I am not getting married", I said, laughing my heart out.

"What is cooking between you and Ketki now by the way?"

"Ahem. It is going good Gauti. Thanks a ton to you again. Now we four can make a good group and hang out", Arush said.

"That is really a nice idea. We will surely plan up something soon. I got to go now", I said and hung up. I had to watch my favourite Bollywood news, which I never used to miss, and always loved knowing everything that is happening and cooking in the Indian film industry. It used to interest me in a very special way, and maybe that was where my eternal connection with it lied. I watched some movies post the news by skimming various television channels and slept off.

The next day after returning from school, I had to go and pick my sister Geetika, from her college. My sister was doing her engineering from a reputed private university in Delhi. She used to commute everyday in our own car and a separate driver was assigned to pick and drop her everyday. Sometimes, when the driver was not free, and if I was at home, I had to officially become her driver and could never say no to my parents too.

I was driving to her college, and owing to general office closing hours, there was heavy traffic on the parallel side of the road. Luckily my car was moving smoothly. My car was standing at a traffic signal when I saw a person sitting in his car in the parallel lane for the vehicles coming from the opposite direction. He was stuck in traffic and continuously honking. I looked at him and as soon as we had an eye contact, I started laughing looking at him.

Since I was in a jovial mood, I was behaving a bit childishly and was not minding it as well. He made an angry faced and I zoomed forward. As I moved ahead, I saw an auto-rickshaw stuck in that traffic too. A beautiful girl was sitting behind in it, wearing miniskirts and busy reading a book. I just looked at her casually. The auto-rickshaw driver saw me looking at her, which was for seconds, suddenly turned back and told that girl something, which I couldn't hear obviously. That girl gave me a "pathetic guy" kind of look and tilted her head in the opposite direction as soon as she heard the rickshaw driver. I got shocked and felt like slapping that rickshaw driver.

"When did the auto-rickshaw drivers start getting so possessive about their passengers? On top of that, when did such pervert drivers themselves become so caring about girls?", I thought. If every person could become like that driver in Delhi, it would no longer be the unsafe city for women as it is deemed to be. As a matter of fact, there were a few bad elements only who had spoiled the name of the city. I reached my sister's college. She was waiting with her friends outside her college premises. She waived her hand saying goodbye to them as soon as she saw our car.

"Vow! What a VIP treatment for me today! My busy brother has come to pick me", Geetika said, as she sat in the car.

Geetika used to call me 'Gauti' as a nickname, and I used to call her 'Geet' back in love.

We started for our home. I was playing slow romantic songs in the car, and my body language would have easily reflected that something was wrong with me, to the people who knew me properly.

"What happened Gauti? I can see a different person right now. A calm and composed Gautam Kapoor sitting besides me and hearing romantic music above that. I cannot digest it".

"There is something which is popping chunks of happiness inside you, which are touching your face again and again", said Geetika, with her eyebrow raised.

"Nothing my dear sister. I was missing you since morning so I am happy on picking you up myself", I said, laughing myself as soon as I said so.

"Gauti! Please don't mess with me", Geetika said, holding my hand and pinching me now. I screamed with a low voice and a smiling face.

"Alright I will tell you. I had a great business plan on my mind and I think it could really benefit us. That is why I am happy", I said, making things up now. Since it was just the start of my relationship with Devika, I wanted to keep it secretive and let some time pass by to be able to tell to Geetika.

"What? Please don't joke with me Gautam. I know you are just making up stuff", Geetika said.

"No, trust me sister", I said. "In that case can you please enlighten me with this plan of yours. I am all ears", she said.

"I was thinking that a separate temple should be built for only the high class people that will provide them with a sophisticated environment like they desire. We can keep our own trained priests over there. Such people will probably donate big amounts, which can be put in our pockets easily. Along with that, we can get their slippers or shoes stolen from the temple too, as their slippers or shoes should be costly and branded", I said. There was a quietness in the car for a while, and suddenly we both burst into laughter. I had just blabbered whatever had stuck me then.

"Gauti! I will kill you. I knew you were kidding with me", she said. We both were chuckling. "Okay I am sorry Geet. You know my interest for movies and film-stars right. I thought of a great plan in order to meet them and get famous. But it is a bit hilarious and unreal, that is why I was smiling and shying to tell it", I said. "And what is that?", Geetika said, very calmly. She had got in the mood to hear my crap. Her time was passing in a good way too. "I will file a Public Interest Litigation against the celebrity I desire to meet in any court, on any issue which I can find in any movie related to that actor or anything related to the celebrity's personal life", I said, again with a giggle.

"What an idea! They will come with all their love and hug you for that right?", Geetika said.

"Although I will lose the case, and they might do something bad with me after that also, I will atleast get the chance to come in the limelight as well as meet them. I will bow down and hold their feet afterwards pleading for forgiveness once I meet them", I said, chortling.

"Gauti please stop your crap now and drive the car", Geetika said, and started fiddling with her phone. As we were about to reach our home, there was a traffic signal where both the red and the green lights were switched on due to a technical glitch. I got confused whether to cross the signal or stop. But being a teenager, who usually have an unusual urge to skip even normal red lights owing to the new found craze for driving, I decided to cross the signal. Suddenly from nowhere a traffic policeman appeared, as if he was spying on and hiding somewhere only to stop me.

"Yes little boy. You seem in a bit of hurry. Come out from your car", the traffic policeman said, as he peeped into my car from my side. My sister was getting out of the car to talk to the policeman, when I stopped her from doing anything being a girl, and told her that I would handle the situation. I got off the car. My only worry was not having a driving license.

"Sir, the traffic light is not working properly. Both the red and green signals were lit, that is why I crossed the signal", I said, making my tone a bit polite.

"Please don't argue with me. Show me your driving license", he said. "I forgot to get my license sir. Since you yourself realised too that I was in a hurry, I forgot to get my license in that same hurry", I said innocently.

"There are no mercies my son. You have to pay the fine for not possessing a driving license, as well as jumping the red light", he said, a bit sternly. "Dad", I said. He suddenly gave a horrified look.

"Since you yourself called me son, I actually felt the same. Both the lights were lit, so the fine should atleast be halved due to that. I really apologise for not carrying my driving license right now. Please forgive me. You are like my dad", I said, with my tone getting more innocent. I took out my wallet spontaneously, and opened it in front of him. I had taken out most of the money quickly before I had got off the car and given it to Geetika.

"I only have three hundred rupees sir. My parents don't give me good pocket money. You keep this please. I will have to stay hungry for the rest of the month. That is fine with me", I said, making my eyes seem teary now. "What happens in three hundred rupees nowadays? Anyways, please don't repeat this again. Drive back to your home", he said, excusing me off the fine, owing to my tantrums.

I drove back home. I went to my room to relax, and my phone rang as soon as I lied down on the bed. It was Devika. I was elated. It was the perfect time to talk.

"Hi my sweetheart. You have such a long life. I was just going to call you. I had gone to pick my sister, that is why I could not talk to you", I said.

"Ah! that is so sweet of you my dear. I am missing you", Devika said.

"I am missing you too. I cannot believe we are dating each other. It was a wonderful night yesterday", I said.

"Yes Gautam. I believe so too", she said.

"By the way, I forgot to tell you that I am flying to USA next month for the wedding of one of my cousins, with my family. I will be back after twenty days", I said.

"Oh really! How come you forgot such a big thing Gauti! Why are you going for so long? I will miss you", she said, sounding a bit low all of a sudden.

"Don't worry baby. They will pass soon. But the good part is that I will shop a lot for my Devika", I said, trying to make her happy. The word 'shopping' always works for girls, and can enlighten one from any type of depression too. Gradually the days passed by, with our talks increasing day by day. We started knowing each other more and more, and the fondness only grew. We met whenever we got time, and hugging her or kissing her always made me feel ecstatic.

My family and me had got the visa for the United States after the process, and the last few days before leaving for the marriage had arrived. I gave an official application in school for the leave and was luckily granted without any hassle. It was the last leg of the eleventh standard , and I would have to sit for the final exams just after I come back from the trip. I was least bothered about my exams getting a bit spoiled, as the excitement for the marriage abroad was much more than the mere eleventh standard exams. Soon the day arrived, and we left for the airport to fly to the States.

I had bid goodbye to Devika by meeting her in the afternoon on the day of departure. I had taken my diary in my handbag along with me, wherein I used to write my poems, songs and short stories in my free time. I had showed that diary to Devika also when I had met her during the day, and she had loved it. The parting hug was a bit saddening for both of us.

We reached the airport, and checked in. I had no idea in the wildest of dreams that my life would change forever in the next few hours.

4

There is a captivating Twist in every Tale

"Sir, we have reached the airport", suddenly a voice came from somewhere.

"Are you mad? I have already checked in and proceeding for the security check", I said.

"Sir! We have reached the airport", the voice came again, a bit louder this time. It was the voice of my chauffeur. Suddenly I woke up from the nostalgic journey rememberance of the most precious time of my life. I came back to my senses, and my eyes opened to herds of people glued to my car from all sides, cheering my name and waiting to get a glimpse of me. I was overwhelmed and goose bumps started coming all over my body again. I was back in the reality where I had become the superstar of the nation, and this was just the beginning.

Amidst high security, I got off my sprawling luxurious car. There were umpteen gunmen surrounding me and making way for me to walk to the airport entrance between the huge crowd gathered over there. I waived my hand to the whole gathering and shouted, "I love you all. Only your love and support makes or breaks any person garnering fame in life. Thanks a ton!".

It was such a wonderful feeling and moment, and this was all I had ever wanted, but could never imagine that I would actually get it.

I took a deep breath and moved inside the airport. I did not have to go through any check in and security check. I walked through the VIP channel straight away to my private plane, which was waiting only for me. I sat in the plane and the pilot was ready to take off for Delhi. As we took off, where the 'we' comprised of me, my pilot, my personal cabin crew and security, I started remembering my journey from where I had left it while getting off the car. Sitting in my chartered flight, I remembered how that one flight from Delhi to New York had changed my life and given me this life gradually I am living right now.

My closed eyes took me to that time again. We had checked in at the airport, and got our security check also done. I was visiting all the shopping outlets one by one at the airport and shopping a bit. My mom and dad were roaming separately and shopping for themselves too. I had always loved roaming at the airports and watch planes land and take-off through the gigantic glasses over there. It always used to make me feel amazing. I was sipping a coffee sitting with Geetika and watching the routine happenings on the runway. I took out my diary and started writing a song which was lingering in my mind since some time.

I had a look at all my previous poetry, articles and songs in the diary as I used to feel nice reading them again and again. They were very close to my heart. Suddenly I saw a famous singer of the Indian film industry sitting just next to me and working on his laptop. I was astonished to see the subtleness and calmness in his body language and adored it. I was also a bit quizzed about the fact that much people were not paying heed to him. I thought that maybe everyone is always busy in their own chores at airports, and I chucked the idea of going and talking to him.

"Gautam & Geetika, come let's go. It is time to board the flight", my dad came and told us, as I was lost in my thoughts.

"Okay dad, we are coming. We will meet you at the boarding gate. Where is mom?", I said.

"She is in that shop down there. I will get her to the gate, otherwise she would exhaust the limit of my credit card. You guys come as soon as possible", dad said, and smiled.

"Yes dad I am just completing writing something and coming. Geetika is sitting with me till then too", I said.

"Gautam! You can write in the flight too son. Why do you always get unimportant things in between? Come fast", he said, and left. Although his tone was soft and his lines innocuous, I wanted to achieve something big in this field of writing so that it is not regarded as unimportant the next time by anyone.

It is not the fault of our parents, but the fault of everyone in understanding the fact that nothing is small or unimportant. Everything can be made as big as the Sun and as important as oxygen. We never realise that the things, habits, hobbies, work which we consider as important or prestigious is made so by we humans only. The extremely prestigious work of being a doctor can be even seen low if a doctor deliberately deteriorates the life of a patient by giving false medicines or for earning money. It is all about the perception and efforts put in consequently. I prayed to God for a bit, thanked him for giving me a wonderful family and life, and left for boarding the flight, oblivious of the fact that I was literally walking towards Nirvana.

We entered the flight, and were greeted by the air-hostesses. We had our seats in the economy class.

We sat and became comfortable. I had taken a window seat since I loved to see the outside world from the top, and used to cherish the sceneries. Geetika had fought with me to sit at the window too, and finally we both were sitting at the window, separating our parents of the boon to sit together on a fourteen to fifteen hour flight to New York. We had a direct flight. My mom was sitting with me, and my dad was sitting with Geetika on the pair of seats just in front of us.

The air-hostess started her routine announcements, which I used to find very funny. I always used to imitate them whenever they portrayed the security check measures in the flight. My mom shunned me from doing so, saying that it doesn't look good, but she had a good laugh at it too. The flight took off, and I dropped a last message to Devika before switching off my phone.

"Hi baby! We have boarded the plane and taking off in ten. I am missing you a lot and hope to see you very soon. Have a joyous stay without me, and don't get sad", I said in the message. She was busy with some of her school related work and studies earlier not enabling me to talk to her at the airport.

I started completing the song I was writing at the airport after the flight took a comfortable position in the skies and the air-hostesses started carrying out their routine chores of giving food and drinks to all the passengers.

"What are you writing my son?", my mom asked, as she saw me scribbling something in my diary.

"Mom I am writing a song which is coming in my mind", I said.

"Awww that is so awesome my darling. I am sure your songs would be much better than the top lyricists in the world", she said, putting her hand on my head and blessing me. I felt really touched and put my head on her shoulders. I was surprised at the contrast between the gestures of both mom and dad, although both never had any wrong intentions or will to criticise. All mothers are truly an epitome of love throughout the world.

"Sir, what would you have to drink?", the air-hostess came up to our seat and asked me, as I was chatting with my mom. I saw both hard and soft drinks on the top of her cart. I looked at mom with a very modest face and made my eyes do the talking.

"Okay, but not more than one drink Gautam, and no whisky or wine. Have a beer", she said.

"Okay mom", I said, delightfully. I whispered in my mom's ear not to tell dad about this. The air-hostess herself opened a beer and handed over to me listening to our conversation.

"Thanks a lot", I said, with a million dollar smile.

"One wine for the lady", I said, with a wink and a stylish tone.

"Gauti!", my mom looked at me with a bit of anger and said.

"Just kidding mom. I love you", I said.

Since me and Geetika were sitting in the same column of seats, I was irritating her after regular intervals by pinching her from behind, pulling her hair and other perturbing stuff.

"Mom, look Gauti is disturbing me since when", she turned back and said. I was laughing.

"Gautam. Please don't irritate my doll", mom said. Geetika had a smirk on her face as soon as she heard it. I was still giggling. We decided to sleep for a while, as it was two in the morning. My eyes opened when the sunlight started shining on my face. I had slept for a good five hours. Mom, dad and Geetika had also woken up a while ago.

The flight attendants were serving breakfast to all the passengers. Geetika thought that we had separated mom and dad for quite some time now, so she called mom to sit on her seat and she came back and sat besides me.

"You will remain stupid only Gauti", Geetika said to me as she came and sat besides me.

"Atleast I should get this much leverage of being a younger brother my dear sister", I said, with a cute smile.

"Don't try to butter me Gautam", Geetika said. I got back to my diary and started writing again. Owing to my fidgety nature and irritation in sitting somewhere for a long time, I decided to get up and take a stroll through the whole flight. I had always been curious and loved seeing what others are doing. As I took a stroll, I reached the end of the economy class cabin. There was a curtain ahead, which indicated the initiation of the Business class. I got a bit tempted to peep inside. I noticed that everyone was busy in their own things and there was no flight attendant around. I also observed that some people were sleeping, some of them reading, and some engrossed in watching movies or other stuff on their screen, in the business class. I suddenly noticed that a couple of seats were vacant. I stealthily went inside and sat on one of the seats quietly. I kept sitting for ten minutes, and totally excited, decided to return back and tell my parents and Geetika about it.

"Geet, I just went to the business class cabin and sat there. There was no one around, and I enjoyed it so much. I remembered the last couple of times when we went together", I came back and said, with my pitch a bit loud. Geetika told me to soften my tone.

"Gautam, why are you doing such wrong things here?", my dad said, as he overheard me.

"You know that if the air-hostess catches you, she would throw you out from there and it would be so embarrassing son", he added.

"Dad I know that. I came back to call you guys along to there too", I said, unaffected by what my dad was telling.

"Are you mad Gauti? We won't do such cheap stuff. And you should also not do so. We will fly again through the business class. You come and sit on your seat", my mom said.

"Mom please let me go. I know what I am doing. I have few plans in mind to evade any issue". "Why would they mind?", I said, knowing the fact that I was acting immaturely, but my heart was forcing me to do so due to my incessant love for pleasure, which was not something unusual.

"Okay you go and sit there. You would yourself come back in sometime or be sent back. Otherwise, if you have a good luck, you can enjoy the rest of the flight. We still have four to five hours of travel time to New York", my mom said. My dad was still being a bit fussy about my going there, but my mom calmed him down and he also left it on me, since they knew that the maximum punishment could be the flight crew sending me back with a bit of humiliation. Since they saw me unaffected by the probable outcomes, they also gave up.

But God had other plans already fixed for me, and only that adamance to go and sit in the business class made me achieve this success today. Sometimes even stupidity, in limits, works in your favour if the day belongs to you. Grabbing that opportunity is in your hand then. I took my diary, went stealthily again when there was no flight crew around, and sat in one of the vacant business class seats.

I had already prepared myself to any crew member coming up and asking me about my real belonging in the flight. I decided that I will act deaf and dumb in front of them, coaxing them to forgive me and send back to my seat.

I was minutes away from ecstasy. I switched on the entertainment system, and started watching movies, which was one of my favourite past time. I played a blockbuster movie of one of the biggest superstars Sameer Khan, who was my favourite actor whom I had adored always. The actress of the movie, Deepika Sanon, whom I had coincidently seen very closely at a party some time back in Delhi was one of my favourite actresses. One of the dialogues of the movie had become very famous and I truly believed in it too. That dialogue reflected the meaning that if one possesses the real dedication and trueness to want something, then every passing second will make you get you desire. They say that if you really want something with a true heart, the whole universe comes together to let you achieve it.

I had seen ten to fifteen minutes of the movie when this dialogue came, and I really believe that this dialogue fits perfectly in my happenings thereafter.

I paused the movie in order to go back and inform my parents once that I am sitting here only and would handle any issue if it crops up.

I was just going to play the paused movie after coming back, when something happened which left me flabbergasted. From the washroom at the starting of the business class, I saw a person coming out. I could not believe my eyes, and pinched myself instantly in disbelief. It was none other than Sameer Khan, one of the biggest film-stars of the Indian film industry. My eyes just got locked at an angle at which I could keep gazing at him, spellbound and speechless. He started walking in the aisle towards me, came and sat by my side. My mouth was still wide open, my eyes had stopped blinking with the fear of losing a glimpse of the superstar, and I was just staring at him with my mind not working as to how to react.

"Hi", he said to me, as he came and sat besides me.

"Is that your seat? Surprisingly I didn't see you sitting here all this while", he added, smiling a bit.

I was just smiling and still looking at him.

"Are you alright?", he said, putting his hand on my shoulder. I came to my senses finally. It was a repeat of that party when I had met the famous actress from this very same movie I was watching right now. It was such a big coincidence that I met these two celebrities only, whom I truly adored the most. I was literally ripped asunder in consternation.

There were myriad questions engulfing my mind and heart. But somehow when things are meant to go fine, they usually do. I had put in my own efforts too for the same. I luckily controlled my emotions, consequently not sounding too immature or funny, and had the best conversation of my life with this true legend of the Bollywood industry.

"Yes sir, yes sir. I am fine", I said, with my voice shaking a bit.

"Are you really the one I am thinking you to be?", I said, with my pitch a bit louder.

"I have no clue what you are thinking little boy", he said and guffawed.

"Are you really Sameer Khan, the superstar of the Indian film industry?", I said, pointing my finger towards the screen where the movie was paused and he was visible in that scene.

"Yes I am that same person as that on your screen. I am glad you are watching my movie", he said.

"Oh my God sir! I cannot believe I just met you. It is a pleasure meeting you and the biggest honour to sit in this manner by your side sir", I said, as these are some particular lines which are meant to be said in these kind of situations. But I actually meant them.

"The pleasure is all mine", he said, with a wonderful smile on his face. I was astonished at the simplicity of this great actor as well as his down-to-earth nature.

"But I did not see you before here?", he said. My eyes bowed down a bit in shame and I did not know what to say.

"I understand how you are here. I am surprised no one saw you. Lucky man!", he said, looking calm and unperturbed by my presence there. Before I could say anything, the air-hostess finally came after ten minutes of absence in the cabin to ask all the passengers for any kind of help.

"Hello sir. I haven't seen you before in this business class cabin. Were you sitting somewhere else?", the air-hostess came to my seat and asked, as she couldn't recognise me as soon as she saw me. Usually after so many hours of the flight, the cabin crew tends to remember the faces of the passengers, especially the business and the first class ones, since they are less in number.

"No he was sitting in the economy class. He is my special guest from Delhi. I totally forgot that he was onboard the same flight. I called him to sit with me", Sameer Khan interrupted and said, as I was going to give some stupid reason. My plan of acting deaf and dumb was far from being enacted in such a situation. I was deeply touched by this gesture of Sameer Khan. I was even more inclined towards his greatness now, which was imminent and clearly manifested.

"Thank you so much sir for such a great help. I don't have words to express. I am indeed the luckiest to have come here in immaturity because I met a great person like you", I said.

"You don't need to be so formal with me. I have this much aura atleast that I can say so to the air-hostess. I had booked some of the seats around my own seat too, to fly more comfortably", he said. I was amazed. Obviously it would not have been a big deal for him even if he had booked the whole flight, and consequently he must have realised this the very first time he must have seen me that I have come from the economy class only and sat there for fun sake seeing it empty.

"I really apologise for this inconvenience sir. I will leave right now for my seat. I am obliged to meet you though", I said.

"You don't need to go anywhere. You should enjoy yourself totally and feel comfortable. I understand your feelings. I was also immature and luxury loving like this when I was young in age. I used to do the same things", he said, with a smile. I was getting more and more comfortable as he was breaking the ice by talking his heart out.

"Your are still very much young sir. I am still very sorry for all this. You have no clue how much I adore you. It had always been a dream to meet you", I said.

"Firstly, don't call me 'sir'. Secondly, I am right in front of you. You can talk your heart out. I don't have any work to be done in the flight. I am bored watching movies or other entertainment stuff too", he said.

"I can't call you by your name sir. I really can't", I said. He interrupted.

"In that case, you should go back to your seat", he said, seeming a bit angry now, although he was just acting, something which was his forte after-all.

"Okay I am sorry Sameer. I won't use 'sir' for you", I said, with a weird facial expression and gathering a lot of courage. God had himself paved the way for me to talk at length with Sameer today. God gives similar life changing opportunities to everyone, but leaves the climax in our hands. I could speak all that had always been there on my mind, express my love for films, my interest & passion to enter this industry and umpteen other hidden desires.

He himself portrayed that he was free to talk, and more importantly, willing to entertain a total stranger. All this was clearly reflecting his true greatness. I guess reaching such a stature is impossible without being so good and great hearted. Having a great heart makes you take numerous decisions personally and professionally, which ultimately keeps you intact on the ladder to success.

"That's like a good boy. So tell me, what do you do? What's your name by the way?", he said.

"Sir, my name is Gautam. I mean Sameer, my name is Gautam Kapoor. I have almost completed my eleventh standard and will enter the twelfth standard soon. I hail from Delhi", I said.

"Oh that's nice! Why are you going to New York? You are flying alone?", he said.

"No no! I am flying with my parents and my sister. They are sitting in the previous cabin. I was feeling a bit restless, so I thought of coming and trying my luck to sit here for a while. I am travelling to New York to attend my cousin's wedding", I said, confused about the facial expression to show.

"Why are you going to New York? How come from Delhi? Since you live in Mumbai", I added, chatting as if I knew him from ages. But today I realise that it was just meant to be that way. He is the closest to my heart today.

"Oh my! You have bombarded me with questions. I am flying to New York for a film shoot. My cast and crew are already there. I had flown to Delhi a couple of days ago for an important wedding ceremony, I had committed to attend", he said.

"Now are you satisfied Mr. Detective?", he said. He was responding so properly to my questions. My respect for him was increasing manifold. I developed a strong conviction in the dialogue now, which was flashing in front of me on the screen as my eyes went towards it for a moment. Had I been in the twelfth standard,

I would have never been able to come for the wedding, and consequently get this opportunity. But my role now was to work hard, act smart and utilise this chance in the best possible way.

"But why are you flying in a flight with all of us? You must be flying everywhere in your own private jet right?", I said, with a bit of curiousness.

"I don't fly by chartered flights all the time. It is costly for me too", he said, chuckling.

"Really? I thought you must be owning a private jet for sure. I intend to own one someday", I said, with a beam in my eyes.

"You will little one. I do have a private jet. But it is parked in Mumbai. The producer of the current movie is paying for our travelling", he said. I could see the sense of humour of Sameer. He was an epitome of a complete package of all good qualities possible.

"I had something to share with you. If you are not bored with me yet, can I go ahead?", I said.

"Yes you surely can. You are not boring me. I am finding it interesting to answer your heap of questions", he said, with the lovely dimples on his cheeks.

"I have always wanted to come in this film industry too. I deeply have this feeling that I belong here. What better can it be to get some work from the God of the industry himself", I said.

"Oh really? No I am no God dear. Yes but I can surely help you. I have such a fervent fan. I should help him", he said. I was elated.

"Thank you so much Sameer. This is my diary. I have written a lot of poems, songs and articles in this. I have always dreamt to be a famous lyricist and scriptwriter one day. I have grown up watching myriad of movies of various actors, umpteen times, especially your's", I said.

"That is great. Show me the diary", he said. I handed over the diary with both my hands as if I was handing him over a treasure. It was my only saviour now. He opened the diary and started flicking the pages from the start. It was obvious that he would have not read each and every word. Getting even this much was a big achievement for me.

"Your writing seems fresh. With some polishing, you can do well. Your thought process is good. I am a bit impressed", he said. I was amazed at his speed of glancing with an amazing observation.

"Only a bit?", I thought. I was being unreal and greedy now I knew.

"That is so nice of you. Thanks a ton. It means a lot." I said.

"But yes, the struggle is pretty long. There is a long way to go", he said.

"So what next?", I said, wanting something concrete to come my way this time. I was constantly praying to God.

"We have around three more hours to land. Why don't we conduct the longest interview of your life today Gautam?", Sameer said.

"I did not get you Sameer", I said. Sameer's body language reflected some crazy thoughts snapping in his mind.

"You have rest of the flight to prove your worth to me. Utilise the time left in any way you desire, and show me that you have got that ability to enter this film industry", he said, with his voice reflecting clearly that he meant business. It was a man to man conversation now. I was baffled for a second. It seemed like a black out now. At the same time I was mesmerised with the opportunity coming my way in such a straight forward manner.

"I am ready sir", I said, after few seconds of silence. I was back to my seriousness. For me at this moment, he was the one who could take me where I want to, so I left the amicability behind and manifested that I meant serious business too. My voice had that confidence and courage to prove my worth to him. Sameer seemed impressed too. It was an obligation that he was indeed doing this for me, and he was very right on his part to make me prove my worth. He must have liked my writings I supposed, owing to which he gave me this chance to proceed ahead else he would have indirectly shunned doing this favour after going through my writings only.

"Your parents won't come looking for you?", he said.

"No sir. They know I am here and they trust my capabilities that I would handle any situation. They did stop me from coming like this, but I was adamant to come. I guess my adamancy proved priceless", I said. My confidence was building up.

"Okay. My questions would not lie within the film background. I would ask anything and everything. Don't treat them as crappy questions. Answer in the best possible way. I want to check your smartness", he said, with a wicked smile. I was ready. My body language reflected the 'Bring it on' feeling.

"Is there a way you can get a knife inside the plane?", he said. I was a bit taken aback hearing this question. It was a totally absurd question according to me. But he had cleared the air on it before starting only. I realised how the latter questions are going to be. I widened my mind's horizon in all directions now.

"We cannot get a knife inside in any way due to the security check. We can although take it from an employee in the various restaurants inside the airport after getting the security check done as they would be using them for cooking purposes. Bribing them and taking it is easier than bribing the policemen at the security check", I said. I was also saying whatever I could think of. Since his questions were also illogical ones, so had to be my answers. The possibility factor of the answer was not the need of the hour, and I had understood this fact. Sameer seemed convinced.

"If you spot a girl driving a car on the road and you find her hot, how would you talk to her? Is there any way out?", he said.

"Don't say that you would just chase her and see where she is going and then try to find out things", he added, laughing.

"I won't do that sir. I would take my car behind her's and bang it from behind. She would stop and come out, shout at me and I would apologise the most sweetly. I would then give her my number saying that I don't have money and promise to give her in a day or two by meeting her wherever she calls me. The talks can then continue once I have her number and I meet her a couple of times", I said.

"Have you done this before? You sound trained for that", Sameer said, giving a smile, and sounding happy hearing my convincing answers.

"Okay. You need to make your parents trust you when it comes to handling money for important purposes. What can you do in the quickest way", he said. I again thought as fast as I could.

"I would ask them to give me some money for some work at the moment they would be busy in their own work. When I would go and take the money from their wallet, I would take some extra money. When I get back, I would tell them that by chance I got extra money with me and return it back. I would even return back the pocket money they give a couple of times telling that I did not spend all of it, so they can pay me less for the next month", I said.

"You seem really smart and prepared. Had you stolen the questions from my mind?", he said, giggling.

"What is more dangerous to my profession? A new actor entering the industry or an already established competitor?", he said.

"Sir, even the smallest mosquito can spread poison throughout the body. Thus, both are equally dangerous. It is just the time factor both would take to pursue the same destruction", I said.

"Oh. I agree. Okay the next one. You love a girl madly. Your parents are not agreeing or approving of her. Rather than running away, or being totally adamant in front of them, or blackmailing to commit suicide, or crying all day, is there any other way left too by which you can emotionally convince them?", he said. I thought for a while and then answered by picking some more answers from my illusionary world. He had removed all possible answers already.

"It can be done, but the method is a bit costly. I can get a clone of the girl made. I can convince any of my friend to wear that cloned face. I can then plan different meetings of that girl with my family which would look as a coincidence, gradually make my family emotional. That would make them think that this should be the will of God so mush so that the power of my love created this situation", I said. I was myself a bit skeptical about the answer. Sameer seemed partially in favour. He was only checking my thinking pattern, my smartness and ability to handle various situations. Writing does majorly involve all possible spans of thinking after all.

"How can you impress the mom of your girl friend in the best possible way?", he said.

"I can plan a mild accident of my girlfriend's sibling or close relative of her mom and save them in a heroic way, swiping her off her feet instantly", I said.

"You have a totally filmy mind Gautam", he said, guffawing.

"I am pretty impressed by your quick responses and thinking, although my questions were a bit absurd. But for these questions, your answers are very unique and perfect", he added.

"Thank you so much Sameer. But I have one question now to ask if you don't mind. From where did you manage to store such questions in your mind and ask so spontaneously", I said.

"I knew you would ask this in the end. Actually all the questions were overheard or asked from me by small kids, here and there, and I had found them amusing. Something, which is striking, does get registered in your mind somehow. I thought it was the right moment to throw them all on you and look at what you say", he said, laughing.

"Oh I see. It's understandable. How did you like my writings by the way?", I said.

"They were pretty good, as I told you. They had a newness in them. So you only want to go into this writing field in the film industry?", he said.

"No Sameer. There is no hard and fast rule. But I want to start off with what I am good and confident at. Rest lies on the polishing of other skills with time, in case I get an opportunity to enter this prestigious line", I said.

"I have always wanted my thoughts to be conveyed to the world. I also plan to start writing a book somewhere down the line. But due to my craziness for the film industry, I thought I can give it much better creativity in all ways", I added. My voice had that thirst and trueness in every line I said. Surely it was leaving an impact on the legend besides me. Somewhere I also knew that he was having a great time pass asking such weird questions and getting entertained listening to my answers.

"That sounds good. Give me your number. I will give you a call in case I find something good for you where you can fit in. I cannot promise you anything, but I liked your confidence and inclination. You truly did believe in that famous dialogue of my movie I suppose", he said.

"Yes Sameer. I still cannot believe I am sitting like this with you. I indeed had the best interview of my life", I said.

"The interview is not finished yet boy. It is not so easy to become a celebrity you see", Sameer said and smiled.

"I am still ready like I was to answer any number of questions you want to ask Sir", I said.

"Great man! I like this professionalism of yours and your shuffling between 'Sir' and 'Sameer' according to the situation. You have a long way to go, undoubtedly", he said.

"I am sorry if there is anything which you did not like Sameer", I said, very politely.

"That is too humble. I like it. So, do you have any girl friend?", he said with a wink.

The talks went on and on. He did ask more questions related to my hobbies, my journey in life till now, my goals, my thinking pattern and everything one can scrutinise in someone. I conversed and answered all with ease. The nervousness factor, which usually deters a lot of people from succeeding in various interviews, was the major factor I left aside in this interview of mine. Henceforth, everyone indeed has the ability to reach where they want to always, if they are able to set aside their fears. My love for the film industry and the inclination to become a part of it helped me impress one of the most impressive men in the country. I never got anything easily. Physical and Mental effort play an equal role, and I had always done a lot of mental effort in order to become successful. But it is a common phenomena that after one achieves something, the world always oversees their efforts behind it.

I gradually thanked Sameer for giving so much of his time and talking so freely. Sometimes in life, unusual things happen only for a reason. Nobody would have even believed what had happened with me. Sameer himself had told me not to tell anyone anything as of now till he calls and confirms for any work he can get for me. That was obviously a cakewalk for him to get me the best of work, but it was only a way to delay things for the moment. He also needed his time to think about it, the pros and cons of relying on me for the work he would be giving, and whether he really intended to help me out. After all, he had just got to know me.

"It was wonderful talking to you. I would get back to you after I get back to India. I guess you would be back by then too. All I can promise you for now is that you do have a friend forever in Mumbai, whenever you come down over there", he said.

"Thanks a lot again Sameer. I am so much obliged. I have no words to reflect the amount of my inner happiness on meeting my favourite actor. I am thankful to you for giving so much of your precious time, beyond my expectations." I said.

"It was a pleasure meeting a lovely person and an ardent fan as you are", he added.

"Thanks for letting me sit in the Business class for so many hours in the flight. It is almost time to land. I should go back", I said.

"Now run back", Sameer said with a smile. I hugged him and went back. I had a different kind of confidence after these couple of hours. This time had literally changed my life. The way I perceived things, the way I thought about people of such stature, the hard work required to sustain and reach scaling heights in life and various other philosophies of life had completely changed in my mind . I had the most unusual and longest interview of two to three hours in a flight.

As I went back, I had a strong gut feeling by all that had happened that I would be getting a chance to write for sure in the film industry. You do get that feeling of nailing something after you do it. I decided one thing very strongly while getting back that I would hide this biggest happening of my life, from all the people I know.

I decided that I would tell my parents and family about whatever had happened with me today only the day I reach at a successful position in this industry, if I do so. I did not know from where I got such an idea of hiding, but the biggest part was that I indeed followed it with too much strength. It was the toughest part to hide such things, but I somehow always managed it. It is all about how strong your intentions are ultimately, and everything can be made possible.

5

A High usually follows a Low

As I got back and sat on my seat, I was literally numb. The cabin crew was already preparing everyone for landing.

"So, you are finally back from your dream world Gautam. I guess you enjoyed yourself thoroughly", my mom said.

"Yes mom", I said, with no interest to answer anyone for the moment. There was a dullness in my voice already. I was trying to sink in everything.

"What happened Gauti? Did anyone say anything to you? You look a bit depressed", my mom said.

"I second you mom", Geetika said. My dad had gone to the restroom during that time.

"Nothing mom. I am totally fine. When I am coming so late at this time, that reflects that I was sitting comfortably there. I am just a bit tired", I said, improving my tone and remembering my pledge to not disclose anything to anyone.

"You know I met Sameer Khan! He was sitting in the same row as mine", I added, with a spark in my voice, in order to change the mood of the conversation.

"What?! Really? I want to go and see too!", said Geetika.

"Oh my God! Really Gauti? That is so great. It is great that your internal craving to meet him must have finally satiated", my mom said.

"Yes mom it was very nice. I loved meeting him", I said.

"I am going to meet him too", Geetika said.

"It is time for landing Geet. They won't allow you to move now", I said. My dad had also come in the meanwhile.

"Mom, Gautam is so mean. He didn't even come and tell", Geetika said, with a gloomy face.

"I am sorry my dear sister. I thought it would look a bit weird if I keep coming and going from and to the business class. Luckily I wasn't caught by any cabin crew", I said.

"You let it be Geet. We will take you and meet him after the flight lands. Don't worry", my dad said, after hearing our conversation and understanding the talks. The flight landed in New York. As we were deboarding the plane, my dad took Geetika a bit earlier than me and my mom to the front of the flight.

There was already a commotion and crowd gathered around Sameer in the flight, as the passengers who were unknown about his presence spotted him while passing through his cabin just before he could get out. I quietly went along with my mom after Sameer left from the flight. My sister had met him and she was pretty happy.

"Gauti! You didn't seem excited to meet him one second time", my mom said, while we were waiting for the luggage at the belt in the airport.

"There was a lot of gathering around him at that time mom. There was no use of getting inside it with so much effort just to catch a glimpse. I had already met him properly earlier while I was seated alongside him", I said.

"Oh! My son sounds mature. I am happy that you met him properly earlier, else you would have gone mad right now", my mom said, smiling.

We left from the airport. I still was not able to sink in the feeling of what had happened with me in the flight. It was seeming like a dream. The excitement of the USA trip had totally submerged and I was only looking forward to getting back to India now and wait for a phone call from the legend. Somehow, I managed to cut the trip with a reflection of being thrilled throughout. The reason I managed to show my zeal throughout was due to the fact that I was indeed enthusiastic about getting back and starting with an unprecedented life that was on my way. I had thanked God every single day of my trip for giving me the best moment to cherish for life. I did enjoy in the wedding with my family as well as other cousins. We roamed in New York too in the free time and I had started building a new dream world of mine wherever I went. I dreamt of my shows being held in the best cities of the world. I tried getting myself down to earth every now and then. Gradually, the trip came to an end, and I was happier while going back than I was when I had landed here.

"Gautam seems so much happy to go back home for the first time", my dad said, while we were checking in at the airport for our flight back to Delhi.

"He is excited to go back and give his exams dad", Geetika said, and started laughing.

"Yes dad, Geet is right. I am missing my studies", I said, with a chuckle. We boarded the flight and as time flew, we were back home. I did not attempt to go to the first or the business class cabins this time while flying back. Luck is also something which does not favour every single time. It is only about hitting the jackpot while it favours, which I had truly done. People don't realise this fact and keep blaming destiny. Every person gets an opportunity to do something outrageous and extraordinary atleast once in life when their luck favours, but mostly people miss that opportunity too due to their inhibitions and other reasons.

I became busy preparing for my school exams after coming back. I had no choice but to study for them. I had nothing to put my career on stake as of now. I used to keep looking at my phone a lot all day, to check for any missed call or message, but there was none. I even forgot about Devika, the girl I had started dating a month ago. I did not talk to her once I was back. The fervour and enthusiasm of finally getting that childhood desire fulfilled mattered more than anything else to me.

"Hey Gautam. Where have you been baby? I have been waiting for your call since the last four to five days. I was confused whether you are back or not", Devika called a week after I was back and said.

"Hi dear. I am so sorry I have been occupied with a lot of things after being back. Yes, I came a back couple of days ago only. How have you been?", I said, trying not show any uncanny behaviour.

"I have been fine only, since you were not there. Let us meet today and talk", she said. Her cheesy lines were not drawing my attention all of a sudden. I did not know what had happened to me.

"Okay dear. I will call you and let you know the time to meet", I said, and hung up. I tried to come back to senses and realise that my expectations could be a bit high and I should try lessening them and prevent a total heart break in case there is no revert from Sameer. I also realised the fact that I was no one to him and there are a lot of chances that he does not make any efforts for me. Taking someone's number is not a big deal. He just had his share of entertainment for the flight. He must be meeting many such people like me every other day. I should not hurt the people who are close to me in this process. But I decided to keep whatever had happened as a secret even if nothing happens. I met Devika in the evening and spent good time with her. I shared my trip experiences, showed her photographs and it was relaxing being with her.

I gave my exams in the coming week and they ended a fortnight hence. I had entered the twelfth standard and had much more responsibilities and pressure than any other phase of schooling. I was trying to think less about what had happened during that flight now. I thought of concentrating on my career than living in an illusionary world. But somewhere in my heart there was a deep feeling, the similar one I had when I was de-boarding the flight at New York that there was something extraordinary in store for me. So much of dedication and hard work till now could not go waste.

I met Arush the same day. I was skeptical about telling him whatever had happened in the flight, but when I had hid it from Devika, there was no logic behind telling Arush that experience also. Due to our exams and other work from school, we did not get time to talk properly till now. I thought that it would be better to be quiet at the moment and wait for something to happen.

"How was your trip Gautam? It seems ages since we met", Arush said, as he hugged and greeted me.

"It was great brother. You look slimmer. I think Ketki is keeping you fit", I said and chucked.

"Please don't ask about my relationship buddy. Ketki is an amazing girl but she is too dominating. I feel like a slave sometimes", Arush said, seeming gloomy and happy at the same time.

"No one is perfect brother. So the only important thing is whether she loves you truly or not. If there is true care and love between the couple, both of them change themselves sooner or later for their respective partner", I said. Arush seemed convinced.

"How were the foreigner girls by the way? Did you get a chance to flirt with anyone?", Arush said, with a wink.

"I went with my family dude. I had to be sane, and I am a one woman man. Devika means everything to me", I said, with conviction. My mind was itself not convinced about this fact, but this line came naturally to me. I felt more frustrated about that flight incident now. It had made me so confused.

Memories can also be pretty dangerous to our lives sometime. I wish there was a technology in which we could erase the memories we do not wish to store in our brains, so that no grudges remain for the bad people and bad happenings ever. Arush and me chatted for long.

I was comparatively free now at the start of the twelfth standard, so I had enough time to give to my illusionary world. Owing to that, I thought that I should think of a way to mint money in this free time by doing totally bizarre stuff. A brilliant idea struck me. I purchased the uniform of a traffic policeman as well as a normal policeman. I scrutinised the city by driving through most of the roads and searched for all the spots where there was no traffic police at all for a few consecutive days.

I inferred that those areas did not have any kind of surveillance, as I had a look all around for any CCTV cameras too. Then one fine day, I bunked from school, went and stood there in the traffic police uniform. I knew that the people get so scared when a policeman stops them that they never ask for the identification card of the policeman. Also, there were umpteen people who could easily be caught everyday on various grounds ranging from lack of official papers in the car to drunken driving. Being a teenager, I was sharper in catching the offence doers, as somewhere we ourselves used to default in some or the other thing a lot of times. I started catching people from eight in the morning till one in the afternoon.

I was successful in my attempt, as I did everything confidently. I shuffled between different places I had identified to avoid being at a single place for a long time, as a precaution. I did this for four to five days and minted good money.

The second plan was dressing up as a normal policeman and catching people drinking in the car in the night. I knew the places where people go, park their cars and drink. Again, the fear factor of the people was used as a weapon against being caught. The money in these cases as bribery or even fine, was much higher. I had earned a good sum of money in a week, owing to my ideas, and I was ecstatic. I was happy with my stint. It was hilarious watching the body language of people changing as they got caught and the types of bribe they offered. I thought that I could do this more, once I need more money. I saved whatever I had earned and kept it aside to use in case of emergency. I knew that whatever I did was unethical and risky. But what goes around does come around, and that was a lesson I learnt in this journey. I was driving to my friend's place in the evening the other day for a get together.

I did not know the way properly, so I used Doogle Maps to find the exact location. I was going as per the route given by the software in the phone. As I was passing through a road, it seemed a bit crowded, with fewer cars and more people on the road. I was a bit traumatised by the visual.

Suddenly from nowhere, two policemen appeared and stopped my car vehemently. I was flabbergasted. One of them ran and knocked at my door indicating me to get off the car. I had no other option but to get down. I was in the same shoes now. In the fear, even after capitalising on that 'fear' factor and earning a week ago, I didn't have the courage myself to ask the policemen whether they were real policemen.

"Hey kid! What the hell are you doing here?", one of the policemen said, with hoarseness.

"I was driving to my friend's place, sir. What did I do? What's wrong in that?", I said, with a shaking voice.

"So your friend stays here? Is she a prostitute?", the policeman said.

"What?! What the hell are you talking?", I said, with a bit of furiousness listening to the crap he said.

"Talk with respect you little lad else I will crush you beneath my feet. The place where you are standing is the red light area of Delhi", the policeman said.

"What?! I was just following the route the 'Doogle Maps' was showing till my friend's place. Please trust me", I said.

"You can tell your parents to trust you after we call them here", he said, with a cruelty in his eyes. I wanted to stab that policeman then and there. But I knew there was no use of calling my parents here. Even though I was not wrong, I did not want a fuss to be made and explain endlessly to a chain of people, which would obviously follow.

"Sir, please forgive me. This is the first and last time", I said repeatedly, and finally got off from there by bribing him with a good amount. I drove off from there, with a gloomy face. Although I was still in profit from the money I had made in the last week, I was disappointed.

I learnt the lesson that what goes around definitely comes around. I also learnt that technology is not everything. Even trusting a person blindly is not advisable in today's world, then how can one trust a software blindly. We should apply our brains also and be alert at all times. I decided that I should not take a path of fooling people to earn myself a living. There are always proper ways to earn handsomely too, which do not involve frauds.

I decided to share all this with Devika. I called her and told everything, while I was driving to the party through the proper route now. She laughed at the first place, but then explained me properly.

"Gautam, I am glad that you yourself learnt a lesson. I know you would never repeat this. I am there with you always, and I am sure you would make it big with your talent. But you are too cute", Devika said. Her laughter always fastened my heart beat.

"Aww thanks a ton baby. I am sure that I would be able to win the world with your support . Winning your heart already makes me feel so", I said. Geetika seemed so touched.

"Let us play a game dear. We would both find flaws in each other and express it. This way we can improve our relation and be different at the same time", I said. Devika started laughing.

"That sounds so interesting Gauti. We would surely play in a while. Before that I wanted to tell you something interesting. A cousin sister of mine got engaged. I felt so amazing listening to the way her fiancé proposed her, that too at her own home", Devika said. She sounded excited.

"Yes please tell me", I said.

"The guy was invited for dinner by my cousin at her place to make him meet her parents. It was an informal meeting, since she had been dating him for quite some time. The guy had already planned the proceedings. When they were sitting at the dinner table, my cousin's fiancé asked her around ten times in front of her parents if she wanted to use the restroom. I fell on the floor laughing when I heard about it, but it seemed so innovative and courageous. My cousin finally sounded something fishy, and went to use the loo. Besides the sink, there was a ring and a card, along with the guy's photograph on the other side of the sink."

"The card read that in case she wants to marry him, she can wear the ring, come and sit for the dinner without telling anything to anyone as of now. In case she does not want to, she can flush his photograph. Oh my God Gautam! I found it so unique", Devika said. I could sense her craving to desire something of a similar sort somewhere down the line from me.

"Yes that is truly inspiring, and moreover courageous to say so in front of her parents. I would do something better for you baby", I said and laughed. We talked till the time I reached the venue, played my game also, and had a great time chit chatting.

6

Smart moves are made by Smart people

I was enjoying the party with my friends at around half past ten in the night, when my mobile phone rang. I was in a jovial mood by now. It was an unknown number. I thought it must be a spam number, but being in a good mood, I did not think of cutting the call and picked it up. Since there was a bit of noise inside, I came out in the lawn to talk.

"Hello", I said.

"Hey! Am I speaking to Mr", came the voice from the other end. I interrupted that person having a male voice in between. Hearing a 'Mr' made me stronger in my belief that it was surely a wrong number. I thought that who would put a 'Mr' in front of my name and talk, that too at this point of the night. Since I was a bit drunk, I was in a convivial mood.

"No you are not speaking to the one you want to speak to", I said, giggling.

"I am sorry. I thought this was Mr. Gautam Kapoor's number", the person on the other line said. I was almost about to hang up without even listening, but I overheard my name a bit vaguely.

"I am sorry. Come again?", I said, with my voice a bit serious now.

"I thought this was Mr. Gautam Kapoor's mobile number sir. I am sorry for disturbing you", he said.

"Oh! I am so sorry. Yes I am Gautam Kapoor only. I thought someone is playing a prank on me. I apologise", I said, trying to cover up and still wondering why the other person was using the terms like 'Mr' and 'Sir' for me.

"Okay that is alright. We understand. Is this the right time to talk to you sir?", he said.

"We?!", I exclaimed, a bit baffled.

"Yes I can talk", I added, as the curiousness was shooting up more now.

"Hey Gautam! It's me here", a different voice came all of a sudden. I was taken aback for a minute. I could recognise and relate to the voice as that of the superstar Sameer Khan, but my heart was not ready to believe and accept it. I was quiet for few seconds.

"Sameer Sir! Is that really you?", I said suddenly, with my voice trembling.

"I told you in the flight also to not call me 'sir', Gauti", the person in charge of the phone now said. I jumped in excitement as I remembered that Sameer only had told me so during that flight.

"Oh my God! I love you", I said without thinking.

"I am glad you remember my voice, rockstar. That was my manager talking to you initially", Sameer said, with a cheerful voice. It sent jitters down my spine. I was so happy I could not express. After more than a couple of months, I finally got the reward I had been eagerly waiting for.

Arush came up to me as I was standing like a statue in the middle of the lawn outside, since it had been some time now since I came out to talk.

"What happened to you Gautam? Come let's have a drink! I have been looking for you all around", Arush said. I did not respond to him and went in a corner to talk in serenity. Arush gave a weird look and went inside. He must have understood that I was talking to Devika, so he did not enquire anything too.

"I am sorry Sameer. I am so delighted by your call", I said.

"I can see that. You are already partying in my call's anticipation", Sameer said and laughed it out.

"I am just kidding. I could hear your friend calling you but you came somewhere in a corner to talk to me instead. Thanks for that", he said. I was amazed as to how can such big personalities be so down to earth all the time. I was satisfied today that my favourite actor and role model was always rightly chosen by me.

"Why are you thanking me and making me feel embarrassed Sameer. I am on cloud nine right now", I said. My happiness literally had no bounds. I was thankful to God for such a wonderful day. Getting caught by the policeman while coming for the party was indeed not an unlucky incident, as I had perceived it to be. It was an indication of something good going to happen. It is our thinking only which makes us negative or positive. Infact, after negativity, only positivity should prevail, but we usually do the opposite. I had the most awaited dream of mine see some light finally after a couple of months. My patience and benevolence had paid off.

"You always do everything you need to do before hand. That is what separates you from the rest", Sameer said, giggling.

"So it means that you do need to be on and over the clouds now. I am messaging you your flight details. You can print your ticket. I am seeing you in Mumbai tomorrow morning. I know it's a pretty short notice period, but please bear with me", he added.

"Oh my God! Really? But I will fly by myself please. I won't be able to accept so much efforts and favour from your side", I said, really feeling touched and emotional.

"You should thank someone else Gautam Kapoor! I am instructing you, so I don't want to listen to any excuses right now. When you become a big person, you can pay me all back. I won't leave a single penny", he said. We both started laughing.

"Whom should I thank other than you? I also had one request as well as query. I do not want anyone in my family to know about this as of now. I will figure out afterwards when the right time should be", I said.

"You should thank your destiny right! Hiding such things from them is totally your wish. If I can help you in any way for doing so, I would try my best", he said.

"You are too good and adorable sir. I still can't believe that you indeed remembered about me despite your busy schedule. I had really lost hope", I said, getting a bit emotional.

"Well, firstly, I remembered your talent. Secondly, when I had entered this industry, someone had given me a break as a junior artist in a similar fashion. That was the major reason to tell you now, that I did entertain you for such a long time during that flight", Sameer said.

"Really?! All I can assure you is that I won't disappoint you or give you a chance to ever feel that you wasted your time by doing so much for me", I said.

"I am sure you won't disappoint me. Anyway, I hope to see you tomorrow. I need to get going for some work", he said, and hung up. I was mesmerised. I went to the bar and drank more alcohol to enjoy this euphoria. Seeing my energy as I joined everyone on the dance floor, they all sunk in the party mood even more.

"Are you alright brother?", Arush came up to me and whispered in my ears.

"Yes I am all-tight dude!", I exclaimed, although I was just pretending.

"I will take you home Gautam. You do not seem fine", Arush said with a bit of anxiousness. Although I was not that high since I had drank very little, I pretended to be out of control in order to leave the party. It was definitely early as it was the birthday eve of my friend who had thrown the party thus there was a lot of time left for the party to get over. But I thought of leaving in time from the venue since I had to do a lot of preparations now. I knew that if I do not pretend to be sloshed, my friends would not have let me go.

Arush bid goodbye to everyone there, and held me from my back with one of my my hands over his shoulders. He took me to my car. He decided to leave his own car over there and drive me back to my place in my car itself. I was happy to see his care and him sacrificing the party for me. I wanted to share the reality with him, but I thought I should first figure out everything and then select the people who need to know about this gradually.

He planned to sleep over at my place only as he would have to leave his car here. But this was an instant obstacle I faced again. I could not have let him sleep at my place since I had to leave early morning and then it would have been difficult fooling my parents since Arush was also unaware.

I decided to behave in the opposite way all of a sudden. I suddenly grabbed his hand, put it aside and stood straight looking at Arush.

"How was my acting brother?", I said, with a smirk on my face. Arush was horrified.

"You seem totally fine dude. Were you really acting till now? But why?", he said, with a big question mark on his face.

"I left the party for you", Arush said, a bit perturbed now.

"I know that my darling", I said, giggling.

"Darling? I am not Devika!", Arush said.

"I am just having fun with you. I know you are not Devika and that is the main reason behind all this behaviour buddy", I said, very softly and sweetly.

Arush was all ears now.

"I think I am in true love with Devika", I said. I was acting at my best to not look fishy in any way and succeed in getting away from the party, alone, as soon as possible.

"Yes Arush. I thought you should be the first person to share this with, since you are sailing on the same boat. I would advice you to do the same and enjoy this night even more, as we are officially out from home. I need to go and meet her, and you can also go and meet Ketki", I said.

"You are so smart!", Arush said, laughing.

"Seems like a great idea", he said, sounding totally convinced.

"Thank you dear. Everyone in the party will think that we both are at my place. If anyone asks you as to why you took your car too and let me drive back, you can tell them that I seemed a fine enough to drive when we came out, and you were behind me all the time till I drove back home", I said.

Anyway, my plan had worked. I sat in my car and drove back home. I reached home and printed the ticket with the help of the details messaged to me. I started thinking about the way to chalk out things for tomorrow, since that was an important part. I decided to tell my parents that I have an extra class due to the twelfth standard. I thought that I will have to build a base anyway if I have to travel frequently like this, in case things work out tomorrow.

Another issue was that of switching off my phone during the flight. It could have been dealt with easily had I told someone about it by diverting calls. I thought that it should not be a problem when I fly to Mumbai since it would be early morning, and my parents or anyone for that matter won't call me during class hours.

According to the flight timings, I would be getting back by seven in the evening to Delhi and reaching home by eight in the night approximately. I thought of a good excuse, but decided to execute it tomorrow only in Mumbai. Telling my parents everything before hand would have sounded fishy. I prayed and thanked God for the new beginning he had given me, and went to bed.

"Hello baby. I am back from the party. I missed you. I have an extra class tomorrow so would be a bit busy. I just need your love and blessings for making a good career ahead", I messaged Devika and slept.

7

Even in the dark, there is always a Light to Delight

My flight was at nine in the morning. I had to reach the airport by eight maximum. I informed my mom about the extra class in the morning as I woke up early. She scolded me for telling her so late about it but I apologised lovingly to calm things down. I also told her that this would be a frequent thing from now on.

I touched her feet before leaving since I wanted to seek her blessings for such a big day. My heart was telling me at every moment to reveal the truth to her at least, but I exercised a lot of determination to hide it. It was a bit weird to take such a decision, but I had somehow pledged not to tell anything about this to anyone, for a reason I myself didn't know.

"From which direction did the Sun rise this morning?", my mom said in an elated manner, when I touched her feet.

"It is my first extra class mom. And this is the ultimate year of the school to make or break my career. I want to seek your blessings for a wonderful year ahead and success in life", I said, with so much sweetness that she could not have doubted anything and all she could do was hug me and give me her blessings.

I started from home. I had also told her that there would be no buses running on the days of extra class, as I used to commute in a school bus. Thus, to my delight, I left from home in my own car.

I had driven for about twenty minutes when I stopped my car by the side of the road. I pushed my seat a bit backwards, and started changing my clothes inside the car. I had put a set of my best clothes in my school bag. As I was wearing the school uniform, I had to change it. I changed my clothes, put on my sunglasses and started driving again. I was a little short of time too, so I had to rush to the airport.

It was a zig-zag drive till the airport. I somehow managed to reach exactly on time, parked my car in the airport parking area and rushed inside the airport. After getting the boarding pass issued and security check done, I started roaming in all the shopping outlets at the airport. I had to take a gift for Sameer, which I had pre-decided. It was the least I could do as a token of gratitude. The money I had collected as a fake policeman helped me out because I wanted to buy expensive for him.

After scrutinising a lot of shopping outlets at the airport, I finally bought a shirt and a watch of luxury brands for Sameer. He would have been the same even without them, but my conscious did not allow me to go empty handed. I boarded the flight to Mumbai. I was getting goosebumps as it was one big experience for me. I was pretty nervous and afraid also since I had hid from everyone at home, and getting caught would invite a lot of unnecessary troubles.

I chanted the name of God as the flight took off. After an hour of take off, my legs suddenly started shaking. There was a strange and awkward feeling that I am really sitting in a flight, unknown to my family. But I held my nerve, and finally landed in Mumbai as the time passed by. It was the first time I was visiting Mumbai. I had always heard so much about it and seen it in movies, newspapers, television and other type of media. But I never knew that I was going to fall in true love with a place much more than I loved the city of my birth- Delhi.

I had messaged about my flight being on time at the same number from which I had received the flight details at the time of take off. As I came out of the airport, there was a person standing at the arrival terminal holding a nameplate with 'Gauti' written on it. I got amused and happy. I went towards that person in order to indicate that I was the same person whose name-tag he was holding. He gave a weird look to me as if he had imagined a girl with that name thinking it to be feminine.

He escorted me till the car park, where a lavish Jaguar car was parked. A person, who looked like a bodyguard, stepped out of the car and opened the back door for me. I sat in the car with the gift in my hand. I was delighted by the hospitality provided to me. It was such a homely feeling. This was the life I had always wanted to live.

As the car travelled through the areas of Mumbai, I started observing each and everything happening around. I was remembering all I had heard about the "City Which Never Sleeps" from various sources. It was indeed a lovely sight to watch umpteen people busy in their own lives, the ruthless traffic, and the differentiating charm about this place. There was definitely something in its air, which had engulfed me too as soon as I had landed. Gradually, I reached the home of the King of Indian Film Industry. I got a bit nervous now.

The car entered a lavish mansion spanning a grand area coverage, no less than a resplendent and breath-taking palace. I was mesmerised. The bodyguard got off the car and opened door for me. I was escorted by him till an area which seemed like a waiting lounge of Sameer's home and he requested me to sit there. It was no less than the lobby of a seven star hotel. I was served a glass of champagne along with assorted snacks as I sat on a couch. I waited for ten to fifteen minutes, and it took me that much time to just observe the whole area and its architecture. A guy wearing a tuxedo entered the lobby suddenly from one of its various entrances and came up to me.

"Sir, you are requested to come with me", he said. I giggled a bit thinking that even after coming all the way from Delhi to Mumbai, he is still requesting me to meet Sameer. I was obliged by the hospitality though.

“Sure”, I said, getting up from my couch. I followed him through the waiting area till a room on the third floor of the house. My eyes were wide open all the way till my destination, admiring everything around. Every single article and every part of the interiors was priceless and sumptuous. It was really a treat to my eyes.

“Sir, you are requested to enter this room. Thank you and have a wonderful day”, he said, and left from there. I was standing inches away from the door. My legs started trembling as I dilly-dallied till the entrance of the room. I stealthily opened the door and peeped my head inside through the shortest opening possible.

“You can come inside with your complete body Gautam”, a voice echoed in the room. I suddenly stood upright, as my head had tilted to a sixty-degree angle to peep inside. I opened the door properly now and entered.

As I entered the room, I saw Sameer standing and facing a huge transparent glass which covered one side of the room with the plush Mumbai sea line clearly visible from there. The grandeur of the room made me spellbound. I realised that the meaning of one word could be so different for everyone in this world. A room as per Sameer was equivalent to two master bedrooms according to me. There was a resplendent bar on one corner adjoining a beautiful and wide seating area, with the opposite side having a pool table and a big projector screen besides it. Sameer turned around. He looked dashing.

“Welcome to my home Gautam. I am glad you came as per my instructions”, Sameer said.

“Home?”, I thought and laughed to myself.

“Why are you smiling Gautam?”, Sameer said.

“A home for you is a palace for me Sameer sir”.

“I am sorry, I meant Sameer”, I said, as I saw Sameer making an angry facial expression on my usage of the ‘sir’ word.

“Thanks a ton for remembering me and calling me here Sameer. The hospitality has been breath taking till now”, I said.

"No life is an easy life dear. The more you achieve, the more you have to be on your toes always to maintain it and flourish it. Nothing comes free of cost", he said.

"I agree to that Sameer. It's easy to envy the goodness in someone's life than imagining the hard work behind achieving that goodness by that person".

"If I may ask, how come you still remembered me? I really thought after a good gap of waiting that you would have forgotten about me for sure, and that was really understandable also. I am asking so because it's the biggest honour to be in the thoughts of someone like you", I said, with my face inundated by curiousness.

"I am cock-a-hoop at your genuine questions and curiosity. You know what to talk and when to talk with the perfect blend. This was one of the reasons that such people tend to be somewhere at the back of your mind", he said. I started blushing a bit.

"Secondly, I remembered your desire and intent to achieve something big with your talent of writing more than I remembered you. Last, but definitely not the least, you have a great destiny which really wanted you to be here", Sameer said. I was flattered.

"You can stop shying and show that grin you are trying to hide" Sameer said, and smiled with his lovely dimples visible now. I could not hold my smile anymore too. It was a thirty-two teeth smile. I was gratified to the moon and back.

I thanked God to indeed give me such a destiny and opportunity to prove my mettle.

"I am dumbstruck Sameer. All I can promise is that I would definitely live upto the expectations you have bounded with me, which indeed made you do so much. I am highly obliged and will never forget this favour all my life", I said, went upto Sameer and hugged him tightly. He seemed happy with my body language and gestures.

"You have a golden heart dear. Don't loose it due to the sheen or shine you see in this world of ours ever, because that is a common thing", Sameer said.

"As far as I am under your guidance and your blessings are with me, I would just be the person you want me to be. I have always given you the place of my role model", I said.

"I thought your girlfriend would be your role model", Sameer said, with his chuckle not stopping. Devika instantly came on my mind. I had totally forgotten about her.

"How you do know that I am dating someone?"

"I mean how can you say that I have a girlfriend? I don't have any", I added instantly, trying to not sound fishy in any way. I thought there was no use of revealing about her, since I had no clue about what our future beheld for us. I had also said no to Sameer on this question in the flight.

"I was just cross checking buddy and trying to know your secrets. You can relax. It is good if you don't have any, you can concentrate in a better way on your work", Sameer said.

"Yes Sameer, I second you. Anyways, I wanted to share a thought of mine with you. People really have such big misconceptions about the film stars and this industry. Although, I never listened to or believed in any, but today, I have truly realised that celebrities are much more down to earth and generous than the umpteen people who would be less successful than all the celebrities are", I said.

"We should never generalise in life", I added, with a thrust.

"I am glad to have come across and met such a genuine and loving person like you. I reiterate that am lucky to have you as my ardent fan", Sameer said.

"Can I be friends with you?", I said, very politely and cutely.

"You already are Gauti", he said, sounding pleased. I felt ecstatic hearing so.

"Let us have a drink and celebrate, and after that we need to get to work. A lot of philosophy has been discussed, and you have a flight back in a couple of hours", Sameer said. We both were served the glasses.

"Allow me to raise this toast to a new and wonderful life with the most wonderful man", I said. Life seemed complete today, irrespective of what my future held for me. We sat on the couch and got to work.

"Okay Gautam, to brief you, initially I would like to keep you undisclosed to the people of the industry, as I myself would want to see your work first and analyse the response of the audience towards it", Sameer said.

"I have a couple of movie scripts to be read and signed by me. It is just in the initiation, so I can recommend you strongly to the music director of the film I agree to do"

"It is really very kind of you to do all these efforts for me. I am deeply touched. I have one more request. If you remember, I had mentioned to you that I want to hide all this frenzy and the new life I am embarking on from my family and friends completely"

"My initial work, even if it does good, would not transform me into a big shot or guarantee that success forever. I want consistency to prevail in my work for some years, which would gradually make me achieve a fame I myself would be proud of. I would want to reveal to everyone about it that day, and if nothing good happens, then there is anyway no use of mentioning to anyone", I said. Sameer could see that I really meant business.

"I like your vision dude"

"I am fine with your thoughts. We can strike a deal with everyone you work with. Suggest me a name to be associated with your work if you don't want your name to be disclosed", Sameer said.

"By GK, for your GK", I said instantly.

"What?! Were you waiting for me to say so and you had already planned to say so?", Sameer said, sounding a bit amused and moved by my reply. He chuckled.

"No Sameer. I had been thinking about it during this talk only and this struck me. I am sorry, I know it is a bit childish", I said, shying a bit.

"It sounds attractive, but it would spark off unnecessary curiosity and can attract legal issues also, although I am not sure of it. I don't want that people are able to think with surety about all your work been done by one person only, and that can safely keep your identity hidden for long.

To solve this issue and also be simple, we can just use the word 'anonymous' for associating all your work with, and that seems perfect to me. Hiding someone's identity in this way is not an issue until any of your work becomes controversial", Sameer said. I adored the thinking pattern of Sameer. This was the reason he was above all. Simplicity is indeed the key to great virtue and elegance.

"Sameer, but gradually as I meet more people in the industry, if I do, and work with different people, won't we have to instruct them all about it? I am myself finding it a bit stupid and burdening you by this weird want of mine, that too when I have achieved nothing. But I am getting a strong desire to disclose myself to the world with a bang only, someday", I said. I was asking for too much without anything in hand as of now I thought.

"See, we have been hiding information about our films, shooting, film-set related pictures and videos for years now till the time we ourselves want to reveal it. There are a lot of people on the sets and around us who work with us, but they all are instructed to keep it to themselves. Nobody is allowed to click pictures and divulge information to anyone".

"But all that is understandable and something which is required. I agree that it would sound a bit stupid to hide your name and face itself, but it is not something impossible. That is really your call. As of now, you concentrate on your work and go with the flow. We can try to proceed in this way. It is all a matter of God's grace on this wish of yours. He has graced you by his blessings till now, and maybe he does ahead also as you work harder and harder", Sameer said. I felt convinced, and left it to God.

"I am sorry for wasting your time on this idiotic issue", I said.

"It is alright. I have been facing a lot of your crap till now. I can see the trueness in your desire, and that is why I am bearing with it", Sameer said, giggling. I started laughing too.

In the meanwhile, my phone started ringing. I was getting a call from Devika. I did not pick it up and put my mobile phone on silent. I suddenly remembered that I have to call my mom also once since I would be in the flight in a couple of hours from now.

"Excuse me Sameer, can I please call my mom for a minute?", I said.

"Sure Gautam", Sameer said. I called my mom.

"Hello mom. I just got free from my extra class. I wanted to inform you that my phone is running out of battery. I forgot to charge it last night. I am going for my engineering coaching class directly from here. I would reach home by eight or nine. Please don't be tensed", I said, keeping my fingers crossed and praying that she does not ask more questions.

"You should not forget such important things Gautam. But it is good that you informed. Arush would also be there in the class with you right?", she said.

"No mom. He has to go somewhere today so he would not be coming", I said spontaneously because I was sure she would have tried his number otherwise.

"Where does he have to go?", my mom said, sounding a bit anxious.

"Mom! Why would I know about his life? In fact, why are you interested in knowing about him? I would be back by eight. I am keeping the phone now", I said, trying to show some anger in order to make my mom not intrude anymore.

"Okay my son, don't be angry. Take care of yourself please", my mom said.

I hung up and looked at Sameer. Sameer was smoking, listening to my talks quietly and laughing on them softly.

Gradually, it was time for me to leave back for Delhi. I bid goodbye to Sameer, who was the sole one responsible for such magnanimity. I hugged him tightly before leaving, and my eyes did become wet. My love for him and the respect for this moment was clearly visible. It was a gob-smacking day for me.

"I hope to see you again soon. I am sorry for taking so much of your precious time today. Thanks a heap for bearing with me and my crap", I said.

"It is alright dear. I had wrapped up my previous projects and had taken a break for a couple of days from work. I was free, that is why called you here. Although all these talks could have been done on the phone, but I wanted you to have a feel of travelling like this for the work ahead. Wait for my next phone call Gautam. Have a safe flight", Sameer said, as I left for the airport. I had handed him the gifts I had got before leaving, and on a lot of his refusing, had forcibly left at his home. I wasn't sure whether he would check them out also or no, but I was happy that I had done my bit and handed them over to him.

8

Life changing opportunities knock at Everyone's Door

I landed back in Delhi. I was numb for a moment, but the reality was suffusing now. I was feeling ecstatic as I went to the parking lot to pick my car and drive back home. It was around seven thirty in the evening, and I was almost on time as per the plan. I switched on my phone now, called my mom and told her that I charged it during the class by borrowing someone's charger and would be leaving in sometime. She was calm about it, and I felt relaxed. But I knew that I had to get down to serious work now and prove my worth.

Having nothing in hand is a big tension, but having a lot in hand is also a big tension. There was a lot of expectation from me by the biggest star of the Indian film industry now, and I did not want to spoil the opportunity that had come my way. While driving back home, I suddenly remembered that Devika had called me and I had cut her call. Surprisingly, she had neither called back nor messaged me again till now. I got a bit tensed all of a sudden. I called her instantly as I was driving back home.

"Hello, who is this?", Devika said, as she picked my phone. I was taken aback for a second, but realised that she must be pissed off and needed some pampering.

"Hello madam. I am an ardent lover of Ms. Devika. I just wanted to talk to her", I said, trying to make her fine.

"Devika does not wish to talk to strangers please", she said. I laughed a bit.

"My dear baby, please don't be sad. I am really sorry. I had that extra class in school I had told you about and then the engineering coaching class. I did not get time to call in between and my phone got switched off when I took out time to call you back. But I missed you a lot all the time", I said.

"It's okay Gautam. I missed you a lot too. Let's meet tomorrow for lunch. It has been so long", she said. I was happy that she did not create a fuss.

"Sure my sweetheart", I said, and hung up. I started thinking all of a sudden that handling Devika would be difficult as I proceed in this new phase of life I have entered into.

"Vow! It is such a lovely and romantic weather today Gauti. I am so glad to see you", Devika said, as we sat on our table for lunch the next day. Devika hugged me tightly before sitting. I was not reacting that much to her gestures.

"What happened to you Gautam? You do not look fine", Devika said. I was silent only.

"What is the matter Gautam? I have been observing you since you have come back from the United States, and I can really see a change in you. Did you meet someone in the flight which has killed your interest in me?", Devika said, seriously. I got alert now. I had a blank look on my face fearing if she had come to know something by any chance.

"I mean have you found someone better than me Gauti?", she said, laughing a bit.

"What?!"

"No!", I said instantly.

I heaved a sigh of relief. I held her hand.

"Why are you even thinking like this Devika? I am just tensed because of my career nowadays. I don't know what will I really do afterwards. I got a scolding from my mom too day before yesterday on the same topic. I need to figure out things for myself", I said, a bit gloomily, as that was the only thing striking me to evade the negative thoughts entering Devika's mind.

"Please don't be tensed Gautam. I am sure God will give you the best. You would really get what you want truly in life and I can promise you that", Devika said.

"That is very sweet of you. How can you promise me so surely ? I told you what I want the most truly dear", I said.

"I am so sure because I had truly wanted you in my life and I got that. I also know that you are a hard working person who will achieve his dreams come what may", Devika said, very politely. I was touched by her care. I was feeling bad at the same time that I had started behaving a bit weirdly with her, which she did not deserve.

"I am so blessed to have you in my life Devika. Give me a hug", I said. I realised that it was totally immoral to leave a person like her. I did love her a lot, but maybe this other gift, which God had gifted me, seemed more precious to me. Having a lot is also a herculean task to handle. I was in school the next day when my phone rang during a class. It was on the vibrating mode, and seeing an unknown number made me go berserk spontaneously. I left the class without even asking for any permission from the teacher.

"Gautam, where the hell do you think you are going like this?", my teacher shouted as he saw me rushing out.

"Sir, it's personal please!", I said, making a weird face and putting my hand on my stomach. The whole class started laughing. The teacher gave me a snobbish look and continued teaching. I was happy I could think of an idea so fast and left the class. I picked the phone as soon as I left the class.

"Good morning sir! This is a service related call from Vodafone. Am I speaking to Mr. Gautam Kapoor?", came a voice from the other side as I picked the phone. I got very furious suddenly. I felt like slamming the phone on the floor.

"No you moron! You are speaking to your father", I shouted on the phone and hung up. I waited for a couple of minutes outside the class, else the teacher would have doubted had I entered back so early. I went and sat on my seat. After a couple of minutes, the phone started vibrating again. It was a different number this time. I got excited again, but then made myself calm thinking that it could be a spam caller too. But my heart was still dyeing to pick the call, as I did not want to miss even the one per cent probability of a call from Mumbai. I could not have run away this time though.

"Excuse me sir", I said, interrupting the teacher again.

"What is your doubt now, Gautam?", the teacher said.

"I forgot my wallet in the bathroom Sir. Please allow me to go and get it, else it can get stolen", I said, with a gloomy face.

"You are really pissing me today. Go and get it fast, and don't disturb me again", the teacher yelled. I ran outside again, and picked the phone.

"Hello Sir. Am I speaking to Mr. Gautam?", came a stern voice from the other side. I was again disheartened thinking that it must be another spam call from someone.

"Yes I am Gautam this side. What do you want?", I said, a bit rudely.

"I am sorry sir if I disturbed you at this time. Mr. Sameer Khan had sent a message for you", the person said over the phone.

"Oh I am so sorry! Please tell me what Sameer sir has told you to convey", I said politely.

"He has told me to inform you about talking to the music director of an upcoming film for the role of a lyricist. He has talked to that person and instructed me to give you his number so that you can talk to him directly", he said.

"Thanks a lot for conveying the message. You can message me the number right away. I will talk to him", I said.

"Sure sir", he said, and hung up. I entered the class with a grin on my face.

"Mr. Gautam, did you find another person's wallet too in the bathroom? The happiness on your face surely reflects that", my teacher said.

"No sir, I am really happy to have found mine, since I thought that it would have been stolen till now", I said, and quickly sat on my seat. I was waiting for the class to get over fast now. It was the last class of the day. I called on the number I had received as soon as I left from school. I decided to go by public transport otherwise the students around me would have heard the talks in the school bus.

"Hello, am I speaking to Mr. Shiv Ghoshal?", I said, as I called on the number provided. Shiv Ghoshal was one of the very reputed music directors of the industry. I felt obliged to be given work by him as a start. But this meant more responsibility.

"Yes, you are talking to the right person. May I know who is calling?", he said.

"Good afternoon sir. I am Gautam Kapoor this side. Sameer Sir must have spoken to you about me", I said.

"Oh yes yes! How are you doing Mr. Gautam?", he said, sounding more comfortable instantly.

"I am doing good sir. I hope I didn't disturb you at this time", I said.

"Not at all Gautam! I just got free from some work. Sameer told me about you and was praising you a lot. Mr. Sameer Khan would be working in this movie and I am the music director for this film. I will mail you the movie script, and you need to go through it. I want you to suggest the songs at some of the scenes I have marked, write their lyrics and send them over to me. Lets see how interesting they can be", Shiv said. It seemed interesting to me. I agreed to do as per his instructions and gave him my email address. I was excited for my first assignment. It was a huge responsibility, and definitely a do-or-die situation. All the love and attention I had got till now from such big personalities would be dissolved into the ground if I don't give my best shot. I went back home and downloaded the script. I was reading it very carefully when my mom came in my room from behind.

"You seem pretty serious for your twelfth standard Gauti. I am proud of you. Study well", my mom said and kissed me on my forehead. I nodded with a smile. It hurt me somewhere to hide this from her, but I wanted to take this pain to give my parents a big smile one day. If the final destination gives happiness to all, the path does not matter that much then.

I scrutinised the script for a week, sent the songs and dialogues according to the requirement of the script, which I could think of after applying my brain for a long time. I thought that there was no harm in sending something extra. I prayed to God that all goes well. It was twelve in the night a couple of days hence as I prepared myself to go to bed. I had sent some days back to Mr. Shiv. My phone rang.

"I was waiting for the right moment till now. This is my private number. You can save it. All the other numbers you have been called from were of my various managers", came a voice from the other side. I was sleepy so I got a bit confused.

"I hope you recognised me Gauti", the person said.

"Sameer Sir?", I murmured, out of the blue.

"Yes it is me only dear. My call timings would be weird like this only always due to the workload", he said.

"What?! That is really you? I am sorry I was a bit sleepy. How come you called me at this time Sameer?", I said, with all my sleep vanished now.

"I called you to give you my personal number buddy. You can save this with my name and contact me on this number. There would be a lot of times I wont be available, but I would surely revert back or message you back whenever I get time", he said, happily. Now you have the answer to my statement in the fight of having a friend in Mumbai whenever you come.

"Thank you so much sir. What made you oblige me so much suddenly sir?", I said.

"Your astounding work. Shiv has praised it to the skies. I am proud to take the right decision regarding you my son", Sameer said. I was captivated and enthralled after hearing this.

"Really? I am so happy Sameer. I indeed have always felt like your son. That is the best feeling. I feel on top of the world that my hard work paid off. I am surprised that Shiv sir went through my work so quickly and informed you also. I though he would revert after a month approximately", I said.

"We are all workaholics dear. It seems like a lavish and charming world from outside, but the hard work put in it can never be estimated by anyone. Nothing comes free of cost in this world Gautam, I told you earlier." Sameer said.

"But you helped me without any intentions sir. I am blessed to get that", I said.

"That was also not free of cost Gautam", Sameer said, and started laughing.

"In what way did I pay you Sameer? In fact I want to pay you back in the best possible way", I said.

"I will tell you someday dear. I loved those gifts you gave to me Gauti, as well as I was entertained on that flight to New York. You have already paid me right?", he said.

"I am glad you liked the gifts Sameer. No, all this is a very small token of thanks from my side", I said, feeling a bit gloomy.

"This is not the time to feel sad. Feel ecstatic about your talent and work. I got to go now. More work would be following you very soon. Welcome to the club!", he said, and hung up. I could not sleep all night in gaiety.

9

Let your Work do the talking

Suddenly there was a great noise and my eyes opened all of a sudden. My private jet had landed in Delhi, and that was the touchdown sound.

It seemed like the longest flight to Delhi till now. I was having a wonderful time memorising all my shaping years. I had not called my parents to the airport to make them avoid the hullaballoo. As I came out of the airport with my security guards around me, a flock of media reporters thronged the arrival terminal along with a huge crowd gathered over there to see me. I felt happy to see such a big crowd after just hours of knowing about me. My vision had paid off. This was the love I had craved for.

"Hello Sir, Welcome to Delhi. How does it feel to become so famous in just one night?", one of the reporter asked.

"Good evening Mr. Gautam. You are the star of our nation. When do you intend to marry now?", another reporter asked.

Numerous questions varying in taste and category were thrown to me. All the reporters were behaving as if they knew me since ages. I was amazed at a lot of questions. I did not even deserve so much of stature right now. Media always creates a hype every where. But they are the ones who have the power to give you incessant fame or defame you. I preferred to be subtle and modest.

"I feel wonderful to be a part of this nation as I have such amazing people around me. I just want to say that this journey would not have been possible without the support of a lot of people and their love. I am indebted to you all. I would be holding a formal press conference soon to answer each and every question you wish to ask", I said sweetly, as my security escorted me till my car. The shutterbugs were trying to capture every move of mine and everyone was cheering for me in enthusiasm. I felt touched by so much love and blessings. I sat in my car and left for my home. I had already instructed for tight security around my home in Delhi, because I knew the press and media would not spare my home also once they get to know I am coming there. I wanted to meet my family in peace.

As my car was passing through the roads of Delhi, I saw a music studio. It made me nostalgic all of a sudden, and I instructed my driver to stop the car there for sometime. I got down, and went inside to visit the studio. It reminded me of my initial times when I had entered the Bollywood industry. Life is always full of these small experiences, which add up to a beautiful journey.

The location of the studio was exotic as it was located in one of the posh areas of Delhi. I used to hang out in the markets adjacent to the studio and shop from there. Luckily, the media reporters were not running after my fleet of cars right now, so I had some time to myself. I had called my parents that I would be coming a bit late. I wanted to spend some time alone also. I was remembering and missing Devika a lot at this moment.

But I knew she would not be there for me anymore, and a call or a message to her number would still and always be unanswered, even after I had become such a big personality today or even if I do all it takes to make up for my mistakes.

I went back and sat into my limousine and made a drink for myself from the bar inside. I sat back and started wondering that if I could weigh all the hearts of the people worldwide and weigh my heart separately, I would really realise with how heavy a heart I live everyday. Today, I had everything I ever wanted, but still life seemed incomplete to me somewhere. So, I wanted that I could really convey the message to people citing my example that money indeed can never buy happiness. But only the person treading on a specific journey can understand it and no one else.

My phone started ringing as I started to get a little emotional.

"I hope you have landed safely son, and I don't want to hear that you are crying due to any reason. You are the prince of India now, and you should be enraptured by your success today", said the person on the phone, as soon as I picked. It was Sameer Khan.

"You have always given me strength and a reason to live Sameer. I love you so much. I should enjoy this euphoria and not think about the past or my deeds. One does not get everything in one life for sure. They say that life is all about moving on, but it is more about not repeating any mistake even for the second time, to live a great life", I said.

"Don't you worry child. Heaven has definitely got a plan for you, and that is why you achieved this fame and stature today. I am sure your life plan is chalked out beautifully", Sameer said.

"Only a person who appreciates and truly enjoys whatever God gives can lead a tranquil life, and you must have realised this strongly after your journey till here", he added.

"You are right Sameer. I would never do anything, which is against you or my family. I should always try to live happily come what may, and learn from my mistakes. I just want that nobody else does this blunder which I did". I said. I got that zeal and strength which had suddenly vanished somewhere, and told my manager to start driving me home. I got shocked after a while when I realised that I had come empty handed to Delhi.

I could not meet my parents in such a way. I knew it somewhere that I had given them the best gift they could have ever asked for today, but the fact that I was still going empty handed to meet them after achieving such a feat was not getting digested by me. It is the gesture that matters all the time, one of the biggest values Sameer had imbibed in me.

I needed to think of an idea quickly which could be executed in the shortest possible time. It was late in the night and all shopping outlets would have been shut down for the day till now. As I was stressing my brain thinking of a solution, I instantly realised the fact that I was no longer a common man, but a big personality today.

I told my manager to get the best shopping stores opened up as soon as possible so that I can go and shop for my family. It was a great feeling to be of this stature today to be able to get impossible things like these done through the contacts I had made. It is just a matter of few phone calls if the network of people you know is good. I reached the mall, which had the best shopping outlets in Delhi. I bought watches, clothes, bags and various other accessories for my parents and sister from the world's costliest brands globally. I had to make up for the last few years also after all.

As I was hopping between different branded stores to buy as much as I could, I remembered how Sameer had got me on a shopping spree after my first work had been adored and accepted by the great music director Shiv Ghoshal. He had made me shop in the same way, although I had bought very few things. I always had a hesitation in taking anything from anyone, but had a giving nature throughout. Maybe those strong core values of not being greedy at any moment of my journey made me reach this supremacy. I left for my home after shopping for my family. I was too happy to be able to give them all this. I was thinking about Geetika's reaction on seeing so many gifts.

My family would already be in a traumatized state after the revelation of my real self today. I was sure they would have discussed by now, the infinite moments on which they would have sensed something weird but could never relate those to the reality. The same would be with the various people and friends I met in this journey at different places. I was just a normal student in front of them, and a rich brat in front of some, depending on what I had portrayed in front of different people.

After my first work had got approved, I was pretty happy due to the praises showered in by Sameer and Shiv. Sameer had to attend the launch of a product endorsement in Delhi during that week only when I had sent the songs to Shiv Ghoshal, consequently enabling me to meet him.

"Hey Gauti. What are you upto?", I got a message from Sameer, a couple of days after I sent my first work. I was sitting in my engineering coaching class when I saw the message. I had finally saved the personal number of Sameer on my phone. I had saved the number under the name of Sameer Khan only, since I knew that nobody would ever believe that it referred to him. My phone started vibrating during the class. Since it was kept on the table, a friend of mine sitting next to me saw the caller's name and started giggling.

"Oh my! Big people are calling my friend", he chortled. I smirked while carefully observing his sardonic expression. If only he knew the truth, I thought and smiled.

"I have saved my girlfriend's number by this name", I said.

"That is a good idea buddy. I can do that too, if I have a girlfriend someday", he said, looking gloomy suddenly. I realised that he must be frustrated due to deprivation of a girlfriend till now. I had to call back Sameer as soon as possible though. I rushed out of the class in the break and called Sameer back. He did not pick up. I had thought the same.

I started feeling guilty of not being able to pick up his call. The class got over in the evening and I headed back home. My phone started ringing, as I was just about to reach home. It was Sameer. I stopped my car in the middle of the road in excitement and picked up the phone.

"Hey Sameer, I am so sorry, I was not able to pick up your phone. I am nothing as compared to you to even say that I was busy. I am so obliged and embarrassed that you called me the second time", I said instantly after picking the phone, before Sameer could say anything.

"It's totally fine with me Gautam, and you should never think this way. Everyone is busy in his or her own chores of life. It has nothing to do with the stature or earnings of that person", Sameer said politely. I was touched by his wise words. He always had so much to teach me, and I was on a constant learning curve since I had met him.

"Thank you so much for this gentleness. What can I do for you my God?", I said benevolently. Sameer laughed at my usage of the adjective 'God' for him.

"You can come and meet me right now. I am in Delhi. I had come here for a brand endorsement shoot. I would be flying back to Mumbai in a couple of hours. I want you to leave everything and come to meet me right away dear", Sameer said, sounding a little bit bossy, but in a subtle way. I guess he had that right on me because of which he was behaving in a free manner. And I adored it!

"Okay Sameer, I will come as soon as possible. You can message me your location", I said. There was a lot of noise all around now, and I shockingly realised after I hung up that I had stopped my car in the middle of the road. Everyone was honking from behind, and I could see in my rear view mirror that people had started getting off their cars now to come and check the matter. As soon as I saw the person driving the car right behind mine get off, I pushed the accelerator with all my might and drove off, as I did not want to waste a single minute in an altercation.

I reached home and changed swiftly. I came to my mom's room to inform her that I was going out. Geetika was sitting there too and watching television. She turned to me as soon as I entered the room due to the strong fragrance of my perfume. I obviously had to look my best when I was going to meet Sameer, or any other celebrity for that matter.

"Look who has entered the room! Where are you going Mr. Handsome?", Geetika said, in an accented tone.

"I am going to my friend's place for a get together. I know him through Arush", I said, blushing and addressing my mom and sister both.

"Every other day a new friend of yours pops up Gautam. What is the name of this friend now?", my mom said, sounding a bit suspicious. I was confident though.

"Mom, please stop interrogating me all the time. I am big enough now", I said, in a loud and strong tone. My mom got upset by my retort.

"I am sorry mom. I meant that I am mature enough to know which type of people to hang out with", I said, respectfully and gallantly. This pacified her.

"I care about you my son. You will always remain a kid for me even after you get married. You still have your entire career to build", she said.

"I know it all mom. I study with utmost concentration during my study hours and you know that. I am getting late. I will come back on time" I said while kissing on the forehead of my sister and mom, and left to meet Sameer.

He had called me to one of the most luxurious malls of Delhi, which was home to the biggest brands of the world. It was a shopper's paradise for those having deep pockets. I called Devika after a while of starting from my place. It had been a couple of days since I had spoken to her properly, after we had met and discussed all the misunderstandings cropping up.

"Hi Devika, how are you?", I said.

"Hey Gautam. I am doing good dear. You have a long life. I was about to call you. Where are you going?", she said.

"How do you know I am going somewhere?", I asked, getting confused.

"I can hear your car's honking as well as the traffic around you. Close your car's windows and then talk", Devika said. I realised it was an obvious guess.

"Before you ask about my destination which would be your next question, I will myself tell you about it. I am going for Arush's friend's party. I had met him along with Arush a week ago, so he invited me to his place this time as well", I said, trying to sound confident. I was skeptical about the fact that Devika had Arush's number and could check with him anytime, but I had to take the risk, and could think of no other person.

"Okay my dear. It is so sweet of you to tell me everything in detail. I miss you a lot. I am done with all my entrance exams now. I am tensed about the results Gauti", she said.

"Awww don't be sad. I am sure you will clear them all. Let us meet soon. Are you sure you want to pursue fashion designing?", I said.

"Yes Gautam. I have always wanted to be a fashion designer, and match the likes of the great designers of the world. I want to open my fashion designing boutiques globally", Devika said.

"Vow! That is such a lovely passion Devika. You never told me about it, even when I told you all I want. You should pursue what you really want", I said, relating her passion with that of mine. Everyone has the right to do what their heart tells is right for them, and not their parents or family. They are always our guide, but can never read our minds or hearts.

"If you are there with me, I am sure we both will reach wherever we want. By the way, I have a good news for you", Devika said, in a cheerful tone suddenly.

"What is that?", I said, aroused.

"You will have to meet me for that", Devika said, this time in a subdued tone. I realised that she was just fooling around with me and wanted me to meet her as soon as possible.

"I will meet you soon dear. Don't worry. I have almost reached. I will talk to you later Devika", I said, hanging up the phone. I called Sameer right after disconnecting the phone as I had reached the mall.

"Hey Sameer, I have reached the location. Where should I come and meet you", I said.

"Come to the top floor of the mall. There is a private lounge of mine named 'Zia' there. My security will let you in when you reach there", Sameer said. I never knew that 'Zia' was Sameer's lounge. They had closed it for the the public today. It was one of the most expensive pubs in Delhi. I always knew that I wouldn't get an entry there due to my age and hence was thrilled to enter it.

I reached there, passed the security, entered the lounge and saw Sameer. He was sitting with a drink and a cigarette in his hand. His style always had a mesmerising charm. I went and hugged him. The lounge had an astounding ambience and was beautifully decorated.

"Welcome Gautam", Sameer said, as I hugged him.

I thanked him profusely for taking out time to meet me during such a short visit.

"I had to meet you dude. I would have called you anyway over to Mumbai had I not been able to come. Shiv had praised the songs you wrote as fresh and awe-inspiring", he said. My face gleamed with pride.

"Thank you so much for giving me this opportunity Sameer", I said.

"You are most welcome. We can have these emotional talks sometime later. I have my flight back home soon, so we should get to work", Sameer said. Before I could ask Sameer what he had called me for, we exited the lounge. I realised that it was only the two of us in the mall. Such was his power that he had got the mall shut for the general public for some time. However, the shops were still open. He took me to a couple of showrooms of different brands to make me shop. I was totally against it but he did not listen to me at all.

"Chill Gautam. I am not going to make you shop like this every time. You gave me a gift when you came to Mumbai and I didn't refuse it, because it is the gesture which matters. This is a gift from my side for keeping up the good work, not letting my faith in you down, and for being the pure person you are!", Sameer said.

I felt stirred from within because of this generosity showered upon me.

"Why did you specifically mention about this pureness factor Sameer?", I enquired.

"I knew you would pick out the odd thing in my speech. I was waiting for my intelligent son to ask me that. Shiv Ghoshal told me that he had offered you money and asked about your bank account details for the work you did, but you refused it saying that you would only do what I tell you to".

"As a student of your age, saying no to a good amount of money, that too for your own hard work truly manifests your selfless nature Gautam. I had sensed this the first time I met you, and that was the trigger for me to help you. I knew my assessment was right after my conversation with Shiv. You are the next superstar of this generation Gautam, and I give you my word for that.

You have proved that it is passion that helps you achieve your dream and not the monetary value attached to it", Sameer said, sounding sentimental. Being present in a mall devoid of people, except the shop keeper was slightly unnerving.

"How will I take so many gifts to my home? If anyone catches me, what will I tell them about how I bought them?", I said, after I gulped in my tears owing to so much goodness around me now.

"You were only adamant to hide it from your family. I had liked your vision and feelings behind this stupid thought of yours, which is why I supported you. You can still reveal everything to them, which you should. You have been successful also in your first attempt and I am sure you are in this industry for good now", Sameer said. His last line made me feel ecstatic.

"You are right Sameer. But I thought about it again. I really don't have the greed for money, because it automatically follows the footsteps of successful people. But I do have the greed to achieve great heights in what I am passionate about, and I feel that I can, with my perseverance and diligence. So I have decided that I will tell my parents and family only when I reach that supreme level.

I know Iam asking for a lot, but I want to see where this wish to keep my identity unknown takes me. I want to be at the pinnacle of my success such that when my identity is revealed, it is with an unparalleled bang", I said. Sameer was speechless again.

"Anyway, Gautam, you will have to fly to Mumbai a couple of times more for some legal formalities, and work along with the singers for some of your songs. I know it is going to be difficult, but this is imperative", Sameer said.

"Is there no recording studio in Delhi?", I asked.

"There are a couple of them, but the main ones are present where I am located. I will talk to the music directors and let you know if your work can be completed by being here, but as you grow and get more work, handling it from here will become a herculean task", Sameer said.

I bid him goodbye, and he left for Mumbai.

10

Never let that True and Unconditional Love go

As the music of the film Sameer was shooting for currently got launched, it got stupendous reviews. The songs I had written were gradually on the top ten charts across all genres. The lyricist's name was given as anonymous. Usually, people applaud the work of the singer and the composer for the song and the lyricist is never remembered or given importance. That helped my unknown identity not garner so much attention at the start of my career in this industry.

"Gauti, have you heard the songs of this new upcoming movie of Sameer Khan? I am in love with them", Geetika said to me, as I was going to bed one fine night. I felt great hearing that my near and dear ones had liked my work too.

I had my pre board exams of twelfth coming up.

Thorough preparation was required for the same. However, my concentration was getting affected due my commitments towards Devika and the film industry. I prayed to God for not getting any call from Sameer till the end of my exams. A call from him would sabotage all my efforts of trying to score well as he would either give me work for which I would not have the liberty of time or call me over to Mumbai. I did not want to let go off academics and put all my eggs in one basket, as there was no guarantee of constant success in Bollywood.

Devika called me up the next day to meet after school. I could not say no to her, else she would have felt bad. I myself wanted to meet her, but I was so much occupied mentally that I did not know where my fondness for her had vanished. She told me to come and meet her at her place, even after I insisted that we meet outside in a restaurant or café. She told me that her parents were not at home and she wanted to spend a good time with me. My mind's horses started running in all directions after hearing this. Instinctively, I thought she wanted to fulfil her desires. However, I started feeling a bit weird as it was sudden and not expected from her side.

I had to make an extra effort to let my feelings flow for Devika as my system was blocked due to numerous other thoughts and feelings. I had a strong inkling that the film industry would become a bone of contention between Devika and me in the coming time. I had no option but to hide the current situation from her as I had not yet told my parents. They had the first right to that information. Also, I did not know what the future held for us. I reached at Devika's place and rang her doorbell.

As she opened the door and saw me, she instantly hugged me tightly.

"I missed you so much dear. This is the first time I have called you to my place. It is because of the surprise I told you about some days back", Devika said.

"I missed you too my baby. You really have a surprise? I thought you must be playing around", I said, thinking hard as to what that surprise could be. After meeting her, I had that magic ignite again, and I thought that utilising her parent's absence for some private moments together must only be her surprise for me. I started feeling enthusiastic now.

"Come to my room dear and let me show you the surprise", she said, with a wink. I felt like being totally naughty with her now. I was happy that I came to meet her, as I was feeling less stressed now. As she held my hand and took me to her living room, all the romantic thoughts popping in my mind got shattered. I saw a girl sitting on her bed. Since Devika was standing in front of me, I could not see that girl's face properly.

Devika slowly turned around, looked at me with a smile and moved aside. I could not believe my eyes. It was Deepika Sanon sitting in front of me.

"This is my surprise for you Gauti", Devika murmured.

"Hey Gautam!"

"You have found a smart guy for yourself Devika", said Deepika.

"Hi Deepika. It feels so amazing to finally meet you. I can't believe my eyes. Thank you so much Devika. You are a sweetheart", I said. I felt enraptured. It was a big moment for me. I could not thank Devika enough.

I felt so guilty for the negative thoughts regarding Devika coming in my mind earlier. She made me meet Deepika, who was a top actress and a good friend of her's since childhood. Devika knew about my passion to meet celebrities and the desire to be a part of the film industry, as I had enlightened her on these realities about my life on a dinner date few months back.

"Aww I am so glad that you loved what I did", Devika said.

"You can pour your heart out to your favourite actress"

I started blushing.

"I had come for the shooting of a film to Delhi few days back. Devika specially pleaded me to come and meet you as soon as she got to know that I am in the city. You are really lucky to have such a caring girlfriend Gautam", Deepika said.

I was dumbstruck. I wanted to bow my head down in front of Devika and tell her how much I respected her love. I also wanted to tell her how bad I had become in the recent days towards her.

"I am obliged that you took out time from your hectic schedule and specially came to meet me on Devika's request. I feel so lucky to have met you this much personally" I said.

I had a good conversation with Deepika. Devika gave her inputs wherever necessary. We talked on Deepika's lifestyle, daily routine and numerous other topics. We spent a good couple of hours chit chatting, post which Deepika had to leave for work. I hugged Devika very tightly after Deepika left in order to thank her. Being in her arms was such a beautiful feeling.

"Why didn't you talk to Deepika regarding getting some work in the industry Gautam? My major motive for calling her here was to let you talk and get you an opportunity to pursue your passion. I wanted you to talk yourself to her regarding this", Devika said, as I hugged her, with a frown on her head. I had a straight face suddenly. I knew that I could not have talked to Deepika about it since the things had started falling into place in a different way and talking to her about it as well would have led a mess.

"I thought it would look cheap and selfish talking to her regarding my own dreams in the first meeting itself. She must be so busy with her own work.

She came to meet us specially, that was more than enough for me dear. I will figure out something myself", I said with conviction, to persuade Devika in my favour.

"Yes I agree with you Gautam. That was the reason why I also did not mention anything to her about this topic, as I thought that it would be asking for too much altogether. I am happy that you also have such high thoughts", Devika said and sat with her head on my shoulders. I felt humiliated by my lies and her framed thoughts due to those lies.

I went back home. I was happy to have met Deepika, and sad to have lied to Devika again. Umpteen permutations and combinations were going on in my mind. Devika was unaware about the other life I had started living. Sameer was unaware about Devika or Deepika being such a close friend to a girl I am dating. Deepika, who herself was a great friend of Sameer was unaware about the lies I had been telling to Devika as well as my recent entry into the film industry. Things seemed getting a bit complicated. I decided to take some firm decisions, which were imperative for the moment.

11

Life is simply what you Make it

Life always has some or the other problems that crop up every now and then that hamper our mental peace. But a happy living is all about not paying heed to the fact that problems are arising regularly, but solving them by taking the best decision at that moment. Those decisions can be right or wrong depending on the priorities and mental level of the person. Thus true happiness and success is retained only in the life of those who realise and learn from their wrong decisions and do whatever it takes to improve them.

I did not think about how Devika would feel, neither I gave importance to my own feelings, because something else was more important to me at that moment. I had to reach a conclusion and avoid the future hassles, although down the lane I absolutely realised how wrong I was. A deep second thought, analysis of the long term view and acceptance to take more pain than the usual is much more important to be on the right track.

I planned a meeting with Devika the next day again, with a will to put an end to the alleged mess as soon as possible.

Devika came dressed beautifully and elegantly like always. She was looking fabulous in a purple dress with tied hair. I was really nervous and trying to gather strength to properly carry out what I had come for today. I had prepared myself mentally with a lot of effort before coming, to not get influenced in any way this time.

"Hi Gauti, you seem more excited to meet me so quickly than I am. I am so glad", she said, as she came and sat.

"Hello Devika. No it is nothing like that. I wanted to talk to you about something important, that is why I had to do so", I said, in stupefaction, with my eyes bowing down.

"Gauti you always make me hyper by behaving like this. I know you just play pranks on me with such acts", Devika said, sounding anxious.

"No Devika. I am serious this time. I am really very sorry, but I am not acting today. My dad got to know about us yesterday, when I was talking to you in the night. I got a serious scolding from him, owing to my twelfth standard exams ahead and lack of seriousness for the same. My mom was also furious on me for dating a girl an year older to me, as it was unethical according to her. Everyone seemed against this relation of ours", I said, with tears dropping from my eyes now. Although the reasoning I gave was weird and false completely, my tears were true owing to the pain of separation.

"I do not believe in whatever they said, but I cannot go against my family. It is the harshest thing to say, but we should part ways now. I really want to stand on my feet now and prove my parents wrong. I would come back to you that day, but I do not want you to wait for me, as I do not want to put an end to your happiness all this while. I want to leave it on God", I said, breaking down completely now.

Devika was numb. She was constantly looking at me without any expression on her face. I got a bit tensed and started shaking her. She suddenly came to her senses.

"Did you hear whatever I said Devika? Are you alright?", I said, softly.

"You are all right Gautam. I am sure you would really be successful in your life. I am really sorry for being a nuisance to you", she said a bit loudly, got up from her chair, and literally ran out of the restaurant with her hands on her face to hide the tears. I so wanted to run after her and make her fine, but I held myself back to avoid the complexities ahead. I lit a cigarette, thinking that it would burn away my pain too. I could not have been be more immature ever.

As I reached back, I entered my home with my school bag, since I had told that I have a coaching class. I was depressed, but I could not show it in front of anyone. My dad was sitting in the lobby and watching television. He had taken a day off from his office. I tried to look normal and entered.

"Hi son, how was your class today?", my dad said, as he saw me entering the house.

"It was good dad. Why didn't you go to office?", I said.

"I did not have much work today, so left it on my staff to handle. You seem a bit sad son, what is the matter?", my dad said. I was amazed that he judged so even when I was trying to look totally fine. It is always tough to fool our parents.

"No dad. I am fine. The pressure of studies is building up, that's it!", I said.

"So why are you taking so much of pressure dear? Just relax and give your exams. You know that I have never cared about the score you get. I believe in you and your abilities. Just enjoy your life and give your best shot", he said.

I nodded.

"Perhaps you should make a girlfriend son. You would be totally fine then. Studies are not everything in life. One should also party and romance to push the stress out. Atleast date one girl before you pass out of your school", my dad said, laughing loudly. I giggled to give a reaction on his words, and went to my room. My heart was laughing and crying at the same time. All the stupid reasoning I had given to Devika was proven wrong to me today itself. Had she heard this conversation of dad and me, she would have abused me all her life, which she still must be doing.

I knew I had done absolutely wrong with her, but I was in a totally confused state of mind. I did not realise what blunder I had committed. The problem with half the population is that they usually get attracted to new people having few or fake qualities, kicking out the people who indeed love and care for them like no one can. I did the same, the only difference being that I kicked out a priceless thing for a price I could foresee I can earn.

My pre-boards were over, and I had faired decently in them. The board exams were round the corner, as well as the engineering entrance exams. I was studying for the school exams one night, when Sameer dropped me a message telling that Shiv had some more work for me now. I was happy seeing the message, but tensed at the same time due to so much lined up ahead. I messaged Sameer back to call me whenever he gets time.

I got a call back from him four days after I had dropped that message.

"Hey Gautam, how are you buddy?", Sameer said.

"I am good Sameer. How are you?", I said.

"I am fine too dude. I am going for a press conference, and you know how the Mumbai traffic is! I thought this is the best time to give you a call. Tell me what is the matter. You are in demand man!", Sameer said, sounding happy.

"Thanks a lot Sameer. I feel jubilant. I wanted to talk regarding some issue I am not able to solve. I have my twelfth board exams as well as engineering exams lined up. I am tensed about managing all the things", I said.

"I understand Gauti. But in the starting phase, when you have finally gained a minuscule recognition amongst few people, it would completely fizz out if you back out. Let me think", he said, and was silent for a minute.

"I don't think I should stop anyone who is willing to hire you for any work in the industry as of now. That would mean axing your own feet. I was anyway thinking this the other day that you would gradually need to travel to Mumbai more often, so either you have to open up about this to your family or I have another plan in my mind", Sameer said, after thinking.

"What is that plan?", I asked, sounding tempted.

"I know the trustees and directors of a lot of engineering colleges in Mumbai. You would have to compromise on the rankings a bit, but I can get you admission in those colleges. You can serve both the purposes then. I will send you the names of those colleges, you can shortlist the one you find the best, fill up its form and give its exam. The board exam's marks won't matter for it anyways now, so just relax and work hard for what you had talked to me the first time we had met in the flight. Nothing should come your way. After all, you left your girlfriend too for the same right?", Sameer said, stressing on the last line with a change of tone.

I was drinking water while listening to Sameer, and the whole water spilled out of my mouth on hearing his last line. I was speechless and clueless for a moment. Sameer started laughing in his iconic style. I was still silent.

"I did not get you Sameer", I said, so softly so that only I could hear it.

"I am Sameer Khan my dear. I have my network everywhere", he said.

"I am sorry Sameer but I am really confused about what you are talking", I said, praying that the matter comes out to be something else only.

"I know you had a breakup with your girlfriend a few days ago Gautam", he said, firmly again. I realised that there was no point hiding it anymore. But what interested me more was that how he came to know about it.

"I am really sorry Sameer that I had hid it from you, but I did not want to tell you about it initially", I said, gloomily.

"Oh my God! That means I was right", Sameer said, breaking into laughter. I was certainly in a big dilemma. Sameer had been dilly-dallying for quite a while now.

"I will die out of curiousness. I am not getting anything", I said.

"Chill Gautam. I was just confirming a half story I had heard by behaving this way with you. You completed it yourself. A very good friend of mine was in the same restaurant as you were that day with your girlfriend. I was just chatting with him the other day when he mentioned to me about an interesting breakup he heard".

"As he was seated on the table next to you, he could hear everything. Eavesdropping is bad, but he said that he started enjoying the conversation after a while, so he couldn't stop it. He told me that he heard some of the funniest reasons by a guy for breaking up, and from all he told me, I gave it a thought that it might be you", Sameer said.

"I am sorry to have hid about it both the times when you have asked about it. I want my focus to on my career, and I know that it would divert me from there", I said.

"No worries Gautam. But remember this for a lifetime that a person who loves you truly can never hamper your happiness or success in anyway. That person will only add to it undoubtedly, and do anything it takes to change the things you do not like in the long run", Sameer said, and hung up. I again started feeling guilty for everything and missing Devika at the same time. As Sameer hung up, I got a call from Arush.

"Gautam, where the hell are you lost man?", Arush said, as soon as I picked up.

"I am here only buddy. Just occupied with studies", I said.

"I know brother. I understand. Same is the situation with me", he said.

"I was thinking of planning a dinner again for the four of us Gautam. It was fun when we went last time", Arush said.

"I broke up with Devika, Arush", I said, sounding low.

"What?! Why?! When?!", Arush said, baffled and astounded.

"It just happened brother. Career is more important, that is all I want to tell you", I said, not willing to entertain numerous questions again.

"I know that. I also think that sometimes with Ketki. But the fact is that she loves me so much, and that feeling is above anything", Arush said. I felt a bit depressed hearing that again. Sameer had just explained me the same things. I did not even have the guts to talk to her or say sorry. I realised that she had not messaged called me even once after that day. I was craving to call her, but I was in deep guilt. I dropped her a message saying sorry for everything, but I knew it would be in vain. I gradually got engrossed in the exam preparations and filling the forms of colleges, especially the one which I chose from the list Sameer had given. I had to fill other forms also in order to show that to my parents. The board exams initiated finally.

12

You are Lucky if you get that Second Opportunity

Two of my exams were left, when I got a call from an unknown number. It was from another music director to whom Shiv must have referred about me. He told me to write a couple of songs on some particular movie scenes about which he briefed me over the phone. I had to sideline my exams and do this work before the deadline assigned. I sent the songs to him after writing them in a few days. I also had to write some lines for a documentary according to the requirement.

'In the serenity of the night when the whole world sleeps,

There is beggar on every other street who weeps,

Life is not the same for everyone even when they all are born in the same way,

For a terrorism, jealousy and poverty free world is what we all need to pray'.

These were a set of lines I had written to be said by the narrator at the starting of the documentary addressing some global issues, which had really impressed the director. I was again applauded for the lyrics of the songs as well as other writings associated with the film and the documentary. That music director had referred me to the director of the documentary after he had received my work and liked it.

All my work till now had been praised and accepted well by the industry. It was not the cliched story of the first few attempts being bad, followed by a comeback and grand success at once. Real success comes in parts, little by little, day by day.

Thus it was not the case that I was getting everything I wanted smoothly. After more than a decade of a desire constantly growing in my heart, after years of hard work in keeping a separate diary and writing regularly in it, after exercising a patience of the highest level, after grabbing without nervousness whenever an opportunity came my way, after letting go a love which rarely comes in someone's life, after sacrificing the comfort of home, separation from family and after being positive come what may since the day I met Sameer in that flight, I got this little success I was basking in today. There was still a long way to go and unprecedented hard work and sacrifices left.

The director had messaged me asking as to why I do not want to reveal my identity even when I am doing so good, and I had explained him in the same way I had explained to Sameer. I had no qualms.

I did screw the last few exams a bit, but I was okay with that. I was positive on scoring a decent percentage in my exams, which would satiate my parents. I got the admission in the college Sameer had referred about, and although my parents were a bit hesitant in sending me outside, they had to. I had deliberately not attempted the examinations of other colleges in a proper way, leaving the college Sameer got me an admission in as the only option. It was not a bad college, thus my parents could not tell me to drop an year also.

"I have been observing you since some time Gauti. You have been behaving weirdly, and you don't seem upset with the fact that you would be going outside for studies", my mom said, a day before I had to leave for the start of my graduation life. I did doubt if my mother had started getting a hint about anything, but I behaved in a proper way to not look suspicious.

"No mom, it is nothing like that. I was just serious for my career, as you have always wanted. I would miss you all a lot, but I am trying to hide my feelings to not make anyone of you feel weak", I said. I was sad indeed to leave my family, but the real stepping-stone to anyone's career is the journey away from home, in an unknown world.

One truly excels in an environment away from home, and that is what coaxes oneself to achieve greater heights. I knew that I was doing this for the good of everyone, although a lot of nervousness encompassed me.

I finally flew to Mumbai for the most important chapter of my life, that indeed gave it a high, which even the oldest and finest whisky of world, won't be able to. The life and people of Mumbai were way different from that of Delhi. The city had so much to teach you in every way. I had rented a flat outside to not be bound by any permission timings of the hostel, although according to my parents, I lived in the college hostel only. They would have not let me stay outside in an unknown city.

I used my savings to pay for the initial rentals and expenditures of a new city. I knew that if I got more work, I would be earning soon too, letting me afford the subsequent expenses. I met the music directors personally for whom I had worked till now after I settled in Mumbai. I had it in my mind that I needed to network well with these people associated with the film industry to get more and more work and recognition. The word of mouth praise for someone spreads in the fastest way usually.

I had less interest in my graduation obviously, so I used to bunk classes frequently. It was a professional world I had entered into, and everything was dealt professionally. I made only a few friends in college deliberately, so that I am not answerable to a lot of people and I am not forced to be a part of their outings and plans owing to my work and requirement of being present wherever and whenever I was needed to. Sameer used to meet me once in a month, whenever he used to be totally free and in Mumbai.

I started earning in good amounts gradually as my value increased owing to my work. My college friends always thought that I am from a filthy rich family, and that is why I can spend so much. I used to party with my friends at the best of clubs and pay huge bills all by myself. There were girls who used to be cajoled seeing my giving nature and charm.

Sometimes, on my special request, a chauffeur driven car of Sameer used to come to my college to pick me up, and everyone used to be awestruck seeing the lavish life I was living despite being a graduate.

As I kept on writing more song lyrics and portions of scripts for different movies, I gained more success and recognition. My name had started becoming a brand, for the film fraternity only, as the outside masses were unaware. I used to fly to Delhi to visit my family once in two months, by booking the tickets myself.

I used to tell my parents that I could book those flights owing to prize money earned by various competitions I kept on participating in and winning. Life was getting shaped the way I had indeed wanted it to. I used to attend lectures and do the film industry work piled up for me stealthily in the classes. A minimum attendance was necessary too after all.

I started getting invitations of various wee hour parties of celebrities gradually, since my identity was not hidden amongst the people associated with the film for which I used to contribute as a lyricist or a writer. But I had made it a point that I do not get any photograph of mine clicked by the paparazzi whenever I used to attend any event or party.

I made so many good friends in the film fraternity, and it was a family away from home for me. Everyone was so supportive and loving in every way, which was the most amazing part. I could never imagine in my life that I would hang out so normally and chill with such big celebrities like I used to do with my friends back home. Mumbai gave me a life I always vied for and used to lure for.

"You know, there should be colleges with smoking and non-smoking class rooms, so that you can study and attend lectures along with a drink or a cigarette in your hand", I said, to a college friend of mine, while we were attending a boring lecture.

"You have a dangerously innovative mind I must say. I second you by the way", my friend answered, laughing it out. I was getting extremely irritated by an extra lecture one fine afternoon, when all these evil and lame ideas were coming to my mind. Anuja, a good friend of mine, was sitting besides me, and I had no other option but to irritate her in return.

"You know Gautam, you are totally like a closed book, whom no one can ever read. It has been six months since we entered our graduation, but still I being your friend, know so little about you", Anuja said. I laughed a bit.

"It depends on the nature of the person dear. I am a reserved type of person. But you would agree to the fact that I have always been there for every friend of mine in need", I said. Anuja nodded.

"What do you think about that guy Anuj sitting in the front row? I have always seen him studying. How can someone be so uninterested in the other enjoyments of life and the opposite sex?", Anuja asked me. This was our favourite past time during class. We used to bitch about the students whom we were not friends with, check them out and find flaws in them.

"You are totally wrong Anu. He is a really desperate guy, who is deprived of girls. He is not able to talk to them, but wants to flaunt in front of everyone that he is a playboy. You would be shocked to hear what I got to know from someone that Anuj once went to a clothing store, and he clicked his own pictures with the mannequins of differently dressed up girls, edited them so that they indeed look real and uploaded on social media websites to gain popularity", I said, giggling.

"What?!", Anuja said, in a high pitched tone. The lecturer saw her, and told her to get out of the class. She could not control her laughter and she went out of the class laughing. The teacher realised that I was also involved in the mischief, and he threw me out too. I was relieved actually. We both burst into laughter in the college corridor when we were out of the class.

"Come let us go outside and chill on the beach", I said to Anuja.

"I think every guy considers every other guy to be an asshole except him", she said, hilariously.

"Maybe, you are right", I nodded.

"Even when your gym trainer trains you so efficiently, that you almost have your abs visible now, you keep saying something or the other to him", Anuja said.

"I do not say so because I dislike him, but because he exceeds the limit of decency. He snatches and puts my phone between the weights of the machine till I complete the number of repetitions he wants, else he knows that even if I get tired once, the mobile phone would be sandwiched by the weights above and below it", I said.

"That is a good thing Gauti. He is responsible indeed for making you so fit, and you still have problems with him. This is what I am talking about", Anuja said.

"Anyways, what do you think about Kavita of our class?", I said, with one of my eye brow raised and a smirk on my face. We both had sat in a taxi and left for a beach in Mumbai.

"She is a bitch!", Anuja retorted instantly.

"See, I can apply your own logic for girls too, that you all are jealous of each other also", I said, laughing it out.

"She has slept with a number of guys Gautam. She blackmails them after that by herself clicking obscene pictures with them, and makes those guys her source of money and a servant gradually", she said. I made a weird facial expression.

"That is so cheap and disgusting", I said. We sat on the beach, and started enjoying the calmness of the sea, with a beer. I felt good hanging out with only some particular people from our college. Anuja had become a true and a great friend over the months.

Since she was also unaware about the other life I was living in Mumbai, she used to consider me as brat, with a heart. She knew that I was innocuous, owing to which she had also developed a fondness for me as a friend. I felt good spending time with her, whenever I used to.

Anuja was a crazy, happy go lucky girl. We had once gone to watch a movie, where the movie theatre was almost vacant as it was an afternoon show in a weekday. She hopped from one seat to another and shouted during the whole movie, as if it was a personal movie theatre. That was the day when I saw that kiddishness with a pure heart in her. Keeping that child alive in you always makes life more interesting.

She somewhere reminded me of Devika too by her habits, owing to which I had always liked her more. I was satisfied though that I had let Devika go at the right time. Being in different cities would have anyways been a herculean task in our relationship if we had been still together.

I found it strange although that she never tried talking again. But gradually as the pain of separation increased, I did realise that whatever I thought was only to pacify my own self and no reason can ever be sufficient enough to justify letting that true and unconditional love go.

I used to miss her a lot but I knew it some where that expressing her all of this would look cheap now.

A lot of times, to play around and fool my friends, I used to sit with them and tell them that I want to become an actor. Everyone used to laugh at me, and I used to laugh stealthily on all of them.

My parents and Geetika had come to visit me for a weekend. I came and stayed with them in the hotel they had booked. I showed them around in the city, since I knew every nook and corner by now, after roaming and partying so much.

"Mom, when are you getting Geetika married now?", I said, to irritate Geetika, as the four of us were sitting in our hotel room after calling it a day.

"She has a couple of years more to live as a bachelorette Gautam. We will not force her in any way. I told you not to irritate my doll", my mom said. I put a finger on my lips.

"I miss you all so much here", I said, as I was feeling amazing lying on the bed with my parents and sister besides me. When you are living away from home, you are always treated like a prince, and same was the case with me.

"He does not miss us mom. He is busy with his friends here and the new life", Geetika said, to annoy me back and take revenge. The talks went on and on and gradually my parents left back for Delhi, after a couple of days.

13

Everything is possible if you believe in Yourself

"You have been doing pretty well Gauti. Now the music directors and even the movie directors approach you by themselves. You are getting paid handsomely now, which would also increase in the coming time if you keep going like this", Sameer said to me, when we met at his home for a party he had thrown for the success of his latest movie.

"I can't thank you enough for this. You were the one who gave me a break. I am just trying to keep up your name by working hard", I said.

"I know dear. I feel proud too. I think you should start writing proper movie scripts too now, and prove your caliber at the next level. This is how you climb a ladder, step by step", he said.

"I was thinking the same a few days ago. I have already started thinking of a good plot. I would write the script in a couple of months and give it to you. The best would be if you yourself produce and act in it, in case you like it", I said.

"I like your confidence man! I am glad that you don't feel hesitant in saying anything. I would love to do that, if the script is good", Sameer said. We partied hard till dawn, and I entertained the celebrity guests with my dance and humorous behaviour. Some people had taken videos and photographs of mine and uploaded at various social media platforms. The paparazzi too had got the chance to capture me in the frame and uploaded on their websites and press releases tagging me as a guest at Sameer Khan's success bash. I just prayed when I got to see them that no one in my family and friends comes across those pictures.

I knew that I won't be able to hide it every time. Unfortunately, Geetika saw those pictures while surfing through the entertainment section of an online news website. Something which you fear from all the time is bound to happen sooner or later. Thus we should never keep fearing one particular thing all the time and instead try to evade it from our heart and mind or find a solution to it. No problem in the world is unsolvable.

I got to know when my mom called me a few days after that success party of Sameer Khan.

"Hello Gautam. How are you doing? How is your college going?", my mom called me and said in the evening. I was resting in my room.

"Hey mom. I am good. I was resting after a hectic day at college. How are you? How are Dad and Geetika?", I said. I always felt lovely talking to my mother. It made me feel at peace.

"Everyone is good dear. We are glad you attend your college lectures also", my mom said, with a slight change in her tone.

"I did not get you mom. I have always been regular in my classes", I said, getting a bit nervous.

"That is great then dear. I thought you have become a star and you only party with big celebrities like Sameer Khan and others", my mom said.

I instantly understood that she has definitely seen the pictures I was fearing about from that party. I started laughing spontaneously.

"Mom! You are such a great actor. Did you see my photographs at Sameer Khan's party? I never knew those paparazzi were real", I said, with a liveliness in my tone.

"How did you enter his party son? You never told us anything about this. From your candid pictures with other celebrities too, it looks like you know them so well", my mom said. She had definitely got suspicious. Moreover, she sounded hurt. I felt very low all of a sudden.

"Yes mom, I had hid a truth from you all. I have made some great friends in my college over the time. I have kept meeting more and more people through those friends. Consequently I keep getting invites for such celebrity parties regularly owing to good contacts which I have gradually made. All the celebrities are pretty down to earth, so a candid photograph with them does not mean that I know them mom. I am really sorry for everything. It just slipped from my mind to tell you guys all this ", I said, sounding gloomy.

"Aww I understand my son. It is alright. I am glad you are having fun and have started becoming mature. I will tell everything to Geetika as she was also angry with you", my mom said. I heaved a sigh of relief. Thankfully my mom did not scrutinise more and believed whatever I said.

I started working on the movie script in full flow in the subsequent days. I started exploring the life of different type of people in the city, grabbing ideas from various places and reading umpteen articles in order to be as innovative and attractive in my first script. I gave it to Sameer after completing it in seventy days. I used to work day and night on the script besides attending lectures and submitting of assignments in the college. The only advantage I had was that of being least serious for college related work, as I did not want good grades for getting a good job or post graduation admission in future.

Sameer loved the idea and the plot depiction of my script. He made me meet official scriptwriters to finish my script in a professional way. I was able to learn at every stage and polish my skills.

I gradually wrote more scripts, and the films made on those scripts earned exorbitant money owing to amazing storylines. The producers used to pay me hugely as a token of appreciation. I had bought a house and a car by myself in Mumbai now. Sometimes, it is only the quality of the work, which makes a person exceptional and not his designation.

Producers themselves started approaching me to write scripts and songs for new movies, which they could produce, in order to ensure good returns owing to my success rate. I gradually started investing my surplus money into different business ventures, which I thought would be lucrative ahead.

I used to enjoy fooling my friends whenever I used to come to Delhi. On one of my trips to Delhi, I did not inform Arush about my presence in the city. I called him up randomly to talk.

"Hey Arush. How are you doing? How is your Economic Honours going?", I said.

"Hi Gautam. I am good dude. Studies are fine. You know how college life is. When are you coming to Delhi?", Arush said.

"As of now I do not have any plans. Today is Saturday night, so you must be going to party somewhere for sure", I said.

"Yes Gauti, I am going to Club MCM tonight. I wish you were here too", Arush said.

"That is great man! Have fun. Don't worry, next time we would go together. I have got some work right now. I will catch you later", I said. I giggled after hanging up.

I got ready for the club too in the evening. I left from my home telling my parents that I am going out with friends. I knew some of the most beautiful girls of Delhi now. Sameer had a home in Delhi too, where a couple of enticing cars were also parked. I used to stay at his place whenever I had to come to Delhi for work without my parents' knowledge.

I parked my own car at his place, drove a luxurious car from there to the club, picking the girls on the way. I entered the club with these extremely pretty girls. I had booked a VIP table for myself, with security all around. Arush was shocked when he saw me with such beautiful models. Since there was security around, he could not come up to me and talk. He called me. I had handed over my phone to the servant at Sameer's home. I had instructed him to cut Arush's phone call and message him back. Arush was stunned to see my message, as he thought it must be me only replying from Mumbai. He thought he saw a guy with a duplicate face as mine. He had his eyes at my table only throughout the party in disbelief. I used to enjoy fooling my friends in umpteen such ways, whenever I used to come to Delhi. In Mumbai, the ways were different though.

Three years hence, I started driving my own enticing cars to my college everyday. I started throwing private parties at my new home I had bought, sometimes for my college friends, and sometimes for my film fraternity friends. The major benefit of having good contacts is that you are able to multiply your profits, as you can try multiple ventures.

From a lyricist, to a script writer, to a businessman was a transition that had not been a cakewalk. Only the person who undergoes the journey knows the obstacles one faces. I had invested my money in a couple of businesses that failed. I lost more than half of the money I had earned in the last five years. I was in a deep shock thinking that all my hard work went in vain. But I never lost hope, and kept the nerve. With the passage of time, I thought of an idea where I started a business related to the film industry only.

I had opened a company, which would cater to recruiting fresh talent, give worthy ones the opportunity to enter the industry, thus creating a portal from where producers could choose different directors, actors, scripts, film crew and amalgamate the best combination together to make a film they want. The portal gave them the costing of different people tied up with our company. My business idea became a phenomenon in the industry.

I could think of such an innovative idea owing to my own problems I had faced till now. Losing your own hard earned money always pinches a lot, thus the humongous loss I had incurred acted as a great support too. Somewhere, I could think of exercising such an idea only because I had the contacts today to take umpteen help the capital to employ manpower to hire the fresh talent and provide all the needy ones great opportunities.

My company gained excessive recognition all over the country, we even went global after being a hit here, and implemented our idea overseas also for the film industry over there. I finally had Hollywood actors and actresses in my list of friends too. I visited a lot of places abroad for setting up the work and various shootings. I used to do all the preparations to make sure that my parents did not call me during those flight hours. I used to talk to them from different cities globally telling that I am in college, or in a lecture, and consequently talk less during the trips.

I also never let my name pop up anywhere as the company's owner and the company was always promoted by its name wherever we went. I had appointed a CEO, who used to handle all the affairs of appearing and presenting before the media. Maybe I still had a long way to go, but considering the time span for which I had been a part of this industry, I had gained much more success than even the new actors. I had umpteen endorsements too.

It was all about utilising my capabilities into different productive ideas and reaping the benefits. I saw true success after failure only, because the dedication and will power to establish a name here kept me going. Although my first song and first script had done extremely well, there was some of my subsequent work that had not fared that well. I had always learnt from every mistake of mine, used to analyse it thoroughly, and not repeat it, consequently delivering the best.

14

For a Great End, you need to be a Great Hearted person

Strange things do happen whenever one thinks that life is going smooth. I had gone to attend a Film Award function's after party in a posh hotel in Mumbai. I was standing at the bar to get a drink, when someone came and patted me on my back. I turned around to find that person to be Deepika Sanon. I was dismayed. I was meeting her for the second time after I had met her at Devika's place in Delhi. In the last few years of being a part of the Bollywood industry, I never came across face to face with her for any banner I had worked under, or in any party or event I had attended. I had spotted her a couple of times, but I had always avoided meeting her.

"Mr. Gautam Kapoor! I finally get the chance to meet the person who has enthralled everybody with his charm, that too being undercover", Deepika said. I was shaken knowing the fact that she knew everything about me, which her talks reflected.

"Hey Deepika, I am seeing you after so long. Thanks a lot for the praise, but how do you know about the reality?", I said.

"Is it so easy to hide such big things dear? I know everything about you. Even the people who have not worked with you but are a part of the industry know that there is a heart throb called Gautam Kapoor", she said. I started wondering as to why she was talking so lovingly to me.

"I know it is not easy to hide such things. I majorly wanted to hide from my family, friends and the masses, which I have succeeded in till now by God's grace", I said.

"How is Devika by the way? I am sure you must not have told her too about it then", Deepika said. I coughed suddenly, to get time to think about the answer.

"She is good. We are not together anymore though. Yes I never told her", I said, with a straight face. I knew I could not hide this thing from her.

"Really? When did you guys break up? She never told me about it. Don't you miss her now?", Deepika said. I could sense something fishy, as to why she was scrutinising, and why was she so interested in my life.

"I do, but I had no other option than to call it quits in order to focus on my career", I said. Deepika started laughing. I was baffled.

"I am sure about that. Have a great life ahead Gautam. Devika still misses you", Deepika said, and went away in a jiffy. I was startled. I was not able to gather what she really meant, but I was convinced that she already knew about my break up, owing to which she deliberately asked me such questions.

"Gauti, come let us roll on the floor", some friends of mine came up to me and took me on the floor. Some models were dancing seductively besides me, and trying to come near me. I was a bit high on alcohol, so I decided to groove with them and got a bit cozy.

"Devika still misses you!"

Deepika's line started reverberating in my mind all of a sudden, I pushed the girls away from me suddenly and went out of the party. Even after almost four years of breakup, I had not been able to feel truly and deeply for any other girl. That too when I have had the privilege to be with the best crowd across the country.

I lit a cigarette standing at the porch of the hotel, and I suddenly started missing Devika a lot. My eyes got a bit wet. I had always tried to keep that wound covered, although it never healed. Sameer was also present at the party, and seeing me walk out swiftly, he also came outside.

He lit a cigarette too, and put his hands around my shoulders.

"I can see it in your eyes Gautam. I know you are missing Devika", Sameer said. I was flabbergasted. My head was already revolving a bit, and it started revolving all the way more thinking that what was really happening. I was amazed about the fact Sameer knew about Devika. I had never taken her name in front of him. I was sure that Deepika must have only told him about it, since they were pretty good friends. But the strange part was the discussion of my life by them all of a sudden.

Before I could say anything, Sameer's car arrived on the porch and he told me to come along with him.

"Where are you taking me?"

"How do you know who Devika is?!", I said. I was not understanding anything. Sameer put a finger on my lips indicating me to keep quiet, and told me to quietly enter his car. I had no option but to follow what he told me to.

We reached Sameer's place. I was still not getting what indeed was happening. As we entered the lobby of the house, I was again dumbfounded. Now, I was totally sane and all the alcohol in my system had vanished after such continuous shocks. On the couch in front of me, were seated Deepika and Anuja.

"What the hell?! How is this combination possible?!", I thought. They both got up seeing Sameer and me, and the three of them started smiling. My face was full of umpteen expressions now.

"So, Mr. Gautam Kapoor, how do you like the plot?", Sameer said, with a smirk.

"I have scripted one of the best stories ever, in the last six years, on your life. What an intense, emotional, career oriented and intriguing love story. I am definitely going to produce a movie on your life

Gautam, which will have the most shocking climax ever", Sameer said.

"I am really not able to understand anything", I said.

"Well, I need not introduce you to my guests present here. You know both of them, and you will know everything soon. Let me begin. Fasten your seatbelt Gauti, as there would be a lot of turbulence ahead", Sameer said, giggling. I was just chanting God's name continuously, and was the most eager to listen to everything. I pinched myself to make sure that I was not in a dream.

"A superstar!", Sameer said, pointing with both his index fingers towards himself, with a wink and a high pitched tone.

"A superstar meets a random guy on a flight, that too a person who stealthily enters the business class. The superstar luckily entertains him for the rest of the flight, does not inform the air-hostess for such an immaturity by him, and listens to his talks. I asked you those stupid questions to pass the left over time as I was getting bored alone in the flight.

But undoubtedly, you had answered well and your work had seemed good to me"

"But that is really not enough my son, to make me call you to Mumbai, set up meetings with music directors, and give you the work you want"

I was looking like a deer standing numb and helpless in front of the leopard.

"I used my contacts to get you an admission in a college in Mumbai, I supported you in a weird demand of yours of hiding everything from your family, I allowed you to use my private jet for flying to different places and I allowed you to drive my sports cars with girls by your side. I know you never got physical with any girl, which is why I always did anything and everything for you"

"Did you never feel Gautam, that how can someone do so much for a total stranger? But this goes without saying that as I got to know you more, you started occupying a special place in my heart", Sameer said, with a thrust.

"I agree to all of this. I always had this somewhere in my mind. I could just believe that you have a great heart, and I have a great destiny. But I always worked hard to keep your faith intact", I said, softly, as I was getting fearful. Sameer started laughing loudly, so did Deepika and Anuja.

"Nothing in this world comes free of cost my dear Gautam. I have always said this to you, if you remember. But you truly have a great destiny, owing to the true intentions behind your dreams", Sameer said, with a tightened fist.

"You know why do you have such a great destiny? You have so because God sent Devika in your life", Sameer said. I could see a beam in his eyes. I was shocked to the core. Before my mind could draw any conclusions, Sameer started speaking again.

"Whatever you have today, this life, this fame, this money, this success, is gifted to you by Devika Goel !!"

"She is the one who has actually paid for what you got for free . She is the one who has loved you insanely since she has met you. She is the one who has really waited for a person who left her by the cheapest reasoning on earth. She is the one who has blindly trusted you despite knowing that you lied to her from the start itself with the story of that girl and the plane crash. She is not dumb, and you are not as smart as you think yourself to be", Sameer said.

I was ashamed and dumbfounded, standing like a statue. The last few statements of Sameer manifested his attachment towards Devika.

"You left Devika in order to reach where you are today, but you never knew that you are leaving a person who is solely responsible for making you reach where you are today. I really have the least role. You always hid everything from her, and she always waited"

"Me and Deepika were shooting for a film in Delhi six years back, when Deepika had made me meet Devika during the free time from our shoot. Devika used to take us to good places in Delhi, since she was Deepika's very good friend and we had a long stay in Delhi. You had no idea ever how deep their friendship was. It was during that time only that she had started dating you, and you had told her about your passion for the Film Industry. During the same time, you had told me the same after you had met me in the flight".

"As soon as she had got to know about such a die hard passion of yours, she had pleaded to me in the most innocent and cutest way to help you enter this film line and give you the opportunity you deserve.

She wanted to give you a surprise by telling you everything, but you spoiled it all before she could reveal anything to you"

"She had told me a couple of times about you, whenever we used to meet, and it was then when I connected the dots and realised that the person Devika had been talking about is the same as the one who had met me on the flight"

"She came to know about it since I had mentioned to her to reconfirm. Thus she has always been aware about everything from the start, your first song, your first trip to Mumbai and every single detail related to you"

"What makes her extra ordinary is that she never felt bad or frustrated that you hid it from her. She always said that it is not necessary that if I love him this way and trust him so much, he would do the same. Her love for you forced me to go out of the way every time to get things right for you Gautam. She has read all your songs, your scripts and knows every detail about the company you started"

"Anuja is Deepika's friend from Mumbai, whom I had personally requested to take admission in your college, in order to test your love for Devika. She used to talk like her, behave like her, because we had taught her to do that. The only reason you are standing at this pedestal today is because you never cheated on Devika, and only focused on your work all these years. Anuja tried coming close to you a lot of times only to test your love for Devika"

"Devika had never approved of Anuja, and she was alright even if you fall for someone else. But my heart never allowed me to see such a sublime love go waste"

"Devika was right that it is not necessary to love a person back who loves you, but when a person loves you so truly without bounds and conditions, not loving that person back and letting that person go is the biggest sin and foolishness one can commit. The pain she has gone through all these years has been the payment for your success Gautam!"

"Everything was planned dear. The tiny flings and flirting you did was all right and not a big deal, as everybody needs a way out to relax. You never approached Devika back again, since you were guilty somewhere, which I realised from your talks, else I would have never done anything for you. You never exceeded your limits with anyone, instead slowly and slowly kept burning from inside due to the pain of separation, even when you could date the best of girls here", Sameer said.

"You told Devika to wait for you till you become something. You are at the sublime point of your career today. Had you told her about this journey from the start, you both could have enjoyed this luxury together and have had a ball all this while. Due to baseless reasons, you yourself let it all go. Still, better late than never"

"The illogical adamance on the fact that you need to leave her was the spoiler. We rarely get such a love in our lives, and keeping them with us only blossoms our life more"

"As far as your work life is concerned, everyone needs to have an aim, desire, perseverance and dedication like you had to achieve anything in this world. You are a great person Gautam. You had a vision, which you achieved"

"It is time that you reveal yourself to everyone now. Devika has forgiven you for your mistakes, because she knows that you love her. She told me to give you a flying kiss before catching the flight. Yes, she is on her way to Mumbai", Sameer said, with a smile and a sigh, indicating completion of a speech which left me speechless.

I broke down, crying recklessly, and bent down on my knees holding my head. I was crying mercilessly, seeing which, Anuja and Deepika ran upto me and tried to pacify me. Sameer instantly hugged me tightly.

"We all love you Gautam. We have always been there for you. You deserve everything you have today, and we have no issues with you at all", Deepika said.

"My best friend Gauti, you look horrible when you cry. Your love is landing soon in Mumbai, so just cheer up", Anuja said, patting me on my back. Suddenly, Sameer's phone rang.

"Devika must have landed. She is coming to wipe your tears Gautam", he said cheerfully, as he took out the phone from the pocket. He picked up the call.

The three of us looked at Sameer with eagerness. He was silent for a moment, suddenly the phone slipped from his hands and dropped on the floor. His hands started shivering.

"What happened?", the three of us shouted unanimously. Sameer picked up the remote of the television and switched it on. His eyes seemed watery. Our throats were choked. He started shifting between different news channels, and we all were shattered by what we saw.

Every news channel was showing the breaking news of a plane crash, which was coming from Delhi to Mumbai. I could not believe my eyes.

"Oh my God! Devika!", Deepika shouted, and burst into tears. We all were crying madly, and I had gone into a deep state of shock. I was cursing myself in the worst possible way. I felt like committing suicide. All the bodies were burnt completely.

"How will I ever forgive myself Sameer? I cannot do this anymore. I am quitting this industry forever, and going back to Delhi. I could not even meet her, say sorry, hug and tell how much I love her", I said to Sameer, as I was not able to stop crying. I started screaming.

"Gautam, I can understand what you must be going through", Deepika said, and hugged me tightly, as she herself was not able to stop her tears from flowing.

"We have lost someone very special. But no one is at fault for what happened. See, you had lied about this incident to her, and it really became true. You have a lesson for your life to learn Gautam. No one can rule over the decision of God. He has made you realise that you can never get a duplicate of Devika again all your life", Deepika said.

"Deepika is right Gautam. You never wanted bad for Devika. But you did some big mistakes which costed her a whole life. She told me before boarding the flight that she loves you head over heels, she was proud of you and about the fact that you also did love her. Your complete hesitance towards Anuja's fake desires whenever she deliberately used to come close to you had given the best feeling to Devika you know", Sameer said.

I was feeling numb, although at the back of my mind, everything, which everyone was saying, was getting registered. I took a break for a couple of months from any kind of work. It was almost the end of my graduation too, and I gave the exams and passed, which was my only aim. I had enough money and contacts to get a degree without even sitting for the exams, but I never used my money for wrong purposes. I was in my house one fine day, packing my stuff to get back to Delhi, missing Devika and crying, when my doorbell rang.

It was Sameer, along with Deepika, standing outside my posh sea-facing penthouse.

"I knew you would rush backs to home after you wrap up your exams. I heard that you have refused to work for a couple of directors who approached you", Sameer said.

"I do not feel like doing anything anymore", I said, gloomily.

"You have to do this for Devika, Gauti. Just think how she would feel, if you leave all this so abruptly. She did so much for you, only to give you what you have. You should respect it, and keep it intact always", Sameer said. I did realise that he was right, suddenly hugged Sameer tightly, and started crying.

"She always knew you loved her. She has seen you work so hard. She would be proud of you sitting above us with God", Sameer said.

"It is time you reveal yourself to the world. Life gives us huge setbacks, but we need to step out of them, and tell the world what we really are. Tell the world about your journey and be an inspiration for them Gautam"

"Atleast you can help every other Gautam to not leave the Devika of his life. You are a strong lad Gautam. If you could leave her because you loved this work more, you should keep sticking to this work, else she would feel the worst", Sameer said, smiling, and trying to make me laugh.

"You know you told me once, that you wanted to have a grand launch event to tell the world who you really are. Let us plan the greatest event ever, spend millions, launch and reveal you to the whole world in the best possible way. This would also make Devika feel the most proud Gautam", Sameer said.

I started feeling better gradually, and we started planning for the greatest launch event to reveal my identity.

Half a year ago, I had decided to try my hand at acting too, after a famous director had approached me for the same script I had written and presented to him. I thought that I could also reveal my debut movie's details as an actor during this launch event.

Ten per cent of the film had been shot, and I told the editors to make a short trailer from that portion to be presented at my launch event.

Anuja was also helping me prepare for the launch event in full flow. Sameer and Deepika used to help whenever they could take out time. I had personally requested Sameer and Deepika to be the host and co-host respectively, of the event. All the influential people of the country, as well as members of the Hollywood film fraternity were invited for the event. I utilised my own contacts that I had built till now, as well as Sameer's deep networking, to call the who's who of the country.

The complete check list of all the work was prepared, sequences of revelation of all the work I had done were prepared, dances were choreographed only for the songs I had written, in order to reveal all my work with a bang. There was a big team working day and night to make the event a grand success, make sure that there are no glitches and ensure the maximum security possible.

We had to take a lot of permissions from different authorities in the country to do a lot of things which were unique and had never happened before.

The event was planned on a Sunday evening to grab maximum audience worldwide, and all the television channels were paid heavily to broadcast only that event, skipping their regular programmes, so that people cannot miss the event if they switch on the television. Professionals prepared different strategies and the big celebrities of the film industry agreed to perform on the stage. The event was marketed in a grand way a the caption that would draw everyone's attention.

'I am the Anonymous', the event's name read so.

I was successful at my attempt to reveal myself as a lyricist, scriptwriter, upcoming actor and a businessman with perfect planning. The masses would have got an exceptional feeling realising the fact that I was the real person behind umpteen super-hit songs and movies which they loved a lot. Everyone present at the event had greatly lauded my hard work and perseverance.

I had prepared a proper speech to keep my audience engaged and tell them about my complete journey to motivate them.

I was standing on the stage, imitating Sameer Khan's trademark style, and took the mike to tell my feelings to the audience and viewers.

"Thanks a bunch for so much love, each and every one of you. I am amazed to see such a love from all of you present here, as well as the people who are watching me on the screen. You guys never knew who I am, but it is only your love and support for my work throughout which kept me motivated.

Thanks a lot to my lovely family and friends for being supportive throughout, even though most of them were also unaware of the path I was treading on since the last six to seven years. I am delighted at the response from everyone out here, and I wouldn't have achieved this feat without the unseen blessings of all you wonderful people.

I want to advice you all to do whatever you feel like doing, but always with that perseverance, without which, you can never really achieve what you want in the best possible way. But in the process of achieving your dream, never let the moments and people you love go away, live every moment completely, because time never comes back, neither it stays the same always. Never let the person who actually loves you go.

I am standing in front of you all today, as a superstar and a rich businessman, but trust me, I am not the happiest person. Money indeed cannot buy happiness, and people need to realise this, because I really have. I have everything I ever wanted today, but still I have a sadness that will always be there in a corner of my heart due to some mistakes I have done. I don't want you to do the same.

I never got the feeling of giving my first earning to my parents, I could never do a lot of things which I felt like doing, even though I was living an ultra luxurious life. In life, it is all about the happiness in what you do. Each and everyone of you is born to fly, you just need to have that vision and work towards it. We all are the same. Everyone is equally capable. I am no different.

I have also realised very deeply in my journey, that every person has a different thinking, and nothing can change that. Life is all about compromising for the ones you love, and not worrying or fighting over their habits which irritate or hurt you. If they love you, they will change for you if you tell them to, sooner or later. You just need to be expressive.

I would also like to communicate to all the masses out there, that you should never make a judgment about something without witnessing the truth yourself. By living the life as a common man before achieving this fame, I realised how much contrasting the image of the film fraternity is set in the minds of people. Living the life as a part of this industry now, I realised that the celebrities are much more helpful and caring for their colleagues than.

I apologise if I have hurt the feeling of any person in any way by hiding my identity till now, but I always had a reason behind it. My journey has not been easy, and I have lost the most important people of my life. I never told my parents about all this also, but their blessings were always with me I know.

I can never thank Sameer enough for what he has done for me. He has always been a second father to me. There are many more people who have infinite contribution, and I would never be able to repay them. One should always be with those people in life who were there with us even when we were nothing.

I hope to keep doing my work in the same way I have done till now. Everything will fall into place for everyone ultimately, but the ones with the least mistakes and regrets will live a more comfortable life.

I want to end by saying that love with all your heart, work hard with all your mind, only be with the people to whom you actually matter, never put money over relations and live a healthy life always"

My show garnered tremendous response. Everyone present there gave a standing ovation after my speech. I controlled my tears, looked up in the sky and thanked Devika.

A huge supportive crowd had gathered outside the ground where the whole event was happening in Mumbai, to cheer for me, and show their love after hearing about my journey, which had been innovatively depicted about in the show.

I also got to know what true love really is! Devika died only because she loved me, else she would have never taken that flight.

But she did the deeds to be remembered forever by the people who knew her. I announced the opening of the largest fashion-designing institute of the country, which was her dream, naming it after her.

My eyes opened suddenly. I had reached my home now. I wiped my tears before meeting my family. There was intense security around my house, as I wanted to meet my parents in solitude. I also had another big gift for them. I had bought and got constructed a lavish mansion at one of the best areas of Delhi. I wanted to take them there personally after meeting them. I had got it decorated like a palace with a big ribbon tied over it in the front.

Devika had taught me a lesson for life, which changed my perception of love and life forever. Life seems interesting to guys when they are playing around with umpteen girls but Life seems a gift to those gentlemen who get a person who loves them truly, deeply and madly.

Life seems a boon to the people who are born with a silver spoon but Life seems a blessing and beautiful to the people who work hard to achieve their dreams.

"Gautam, you have given us the best surprise anyone can. We are so proud to be your parents today", my mom said, as soon as she saw me getting out of the car. She was standing and waiting at the door for me, drenched in sweat and emotions. She hugged me tightly, followed by the other members of my family.

"Gauti! My naughty little brother, you hid all this so smartly from me too. I love you so much. You really deserved this. We all are speechless and still not able to sink in the reality. Just give me your credit card now, and you can go and rest", Geetika said, having tears in her eyes, a smile on her face, and a high pitched tone. My dad said nothing but just hugged me tightly. A father always loves his children without expressing much, but his actions are enough to judge what is inside his heart.

I was touched to see my family so overwhelmed and happy, which although was obvious, but I was apprehensive about their behaviour towards me after such a shocking revelation.

Life went on smoothly thereafter, and I kept on climbing the ladders of success. Whatever I did, and whatever I got, was not something which others could not. A good destiny comes only to those who believe madly in what they want to achieve and work hard for it, which I always did. I did not love Devika with the same passion with which I wanted to become a superstar in the film industry, and that is why I achieved the one which I had pursued with true dedication.

Everyone has that chance to love with true dedication and work with the same dedication, because both are imperative for a happy and successful life.

Life changes every second. It is all about that one day, that one person, that one moment, that one love, that one event, which we will truly cherish forever. The list goes on. But that 'one' thing comes into our life only due to that true intention to want it.

We should never let that true love go because we can never enjoy fame or success alone.

The actual identification of True Love is finding a person who is more concerned about our career and work life than we are. Everyone will have umpteen people in their lives who will claim themselves as true lovers, but they all would be interested in only the fun element of the relationship.

You love someone truly only when you never leave that person by saying sorry. True love for something or someone is always accompanied by immense strength which makes you strong enough to fight any obstacle. I realised my mistake when it was too late, and was punished in the worst way for it. For something I desired truly and thus never left it despite a zillion obstacles, I was awarded in the best way for it ultimately.

In the end, we all become a story, so we should write the best one. We can do that by a strong belief that the size of our audience should not matter to us, and we only need to keep up the good work. In the process, we would actually witness that everything will fall into place.